THE RIVER, THE TOWN

THE RIVER,
THE TOWN

— A NOVEL —

FARAH ALI

DZANC
BOOKS

DZANC
BOOKS

2580 Craig Rd.
Ann Arbor, MI 48103
www.dzancbooks.org

Library of Congress Cataloging-in-Publication Data Available Upon Request

ISBN: 9781950539888
First US edition: October 2023
Interior design by Michelle Dotter
Cover by Jade They

Printed in the United States of America

10   9   8   7   6   5   4   3   2   1

BAADAL, 1995

1

THE RIVER

KAWSAR, JUMAN, AND I are standing on the roof of our school, throwing small rocks at the dish antenna on top of Mohsin sahab's bare brick house across the narrow alley. We shade our eyes from the sun and track each rock's flight. It's Juman's turn and he throws one, with a sharp movement of the wrist, and it goes in. He hurls the next one too hard and it bounces off.

"How many channels do you think he gets?" I ask.

Kawsar shrugs. "Maybe ten."

"He paid half for that thing, would you believe it," Juman says. He lifts his shirt and wipes his face with the hem. "Charged double from everyone at the water station, said we have no idea how much tankers cost, he's practically doing charity, paying for half of it out of his pocket. Made my father pay almost triple. A thief and a liar."

The sun is above my head, burning my hair. Kawsar throws a rock but it is a tired attempt; the heat is draining our energy fast.

"Maybe we should just go ahead and break the dish," Juman says. In his hand is a brick. He raises it to his shoulder.

Kawsar stands straighter, trying to look concerned about being caught and not about the act of wrong, trying to speak casually. "Come on, he's going to find out we did it."

For a moment he and I watch Juman, who glances at us in turn. Then he laughs and says, "You two are cowards. My most trusted friends, my jigar, are cowards." But he lowers his arm, and Kawsar and I grin and thump Juman's shoulder. We go down the stairs, past the classroom where children are gazing dully at the science teacher, and out through the small gate.

Our Town is shaped like an oval with wavy edges. At least that is what it looks like in the picture in last year's geography book, which came for us from the City. The Town is connected to the City by a road which is some thirty kilometers long. A lot of us go there for jobs. We are construction workers, maasi, sweepers, gutter-cleaners, bus drivers, rickshaw drivers, cooks. The Town is considered part of the City but it is also not a part of it because we can do almost everything ourselves. There is a primary school here and a secondary school, a hospital, a pharmacy, though the sizes of all of these have been slowly shrinking. The only thing we really need from outside is water.

About two weeks ago, a three-year-old boy here died. He was some milkman's son so we treated it like a small, sad, forgettable piece of news. Today, a teacher in class six fell down in a faint. The children told us her head went thump on the ground. Another teacher had to leave his class and take Mrs. Zeenat to the hospital because he also drives the school van. And the principal, an old lady with thick glasses on a sagging face, had to go with them to make sure Mrs. Zeenat didn't end up like the milkman's boy. After that, the teachers didn't feel like teaching and told us school was over for the day, which is why Juman, Kawsar, and I are in the big park now.

When we were children, we used to go to the playground which has a swing set, a slide, and a merry-go-round. But now that we are older we prefer to be by the Bara Darya. The name comes from a very long time ago when the river used to be wide and deep. I have always seen it as a thin stream flowing weakly over the ground. When my friend Juman is extra hungry he says it looks like a gray intestine.

It is a warm afternoon but we run until we reach it, and then we go down the incline onto the hard, dried ground, toward the stream.

"I think Aab likes me," Juman says.

Kawsar laughs at him. "You think everyone likes you," he says.

"She said I could copy her math work."

We are by the water. We are running again, not talking anymore. After two kilometers or so we stop but the stream goes on. We turn around and walk, stopping to scoop water into our mouths when we are thirsty. We will try not to be thirsty at our homes, the water there is too little. This week, only one tanker has come to the Town, and the driver said each person could not take more than twenty liters.

At home is my mother, sharp and thin as a knife. She crosses her arms and asks me where I was. Her tone makes me shrink inside; I hate having the same reaction to her voice at seventeen as I had at seven.

"Just out with my friends," I tell her.

I don't look at her face because I know all its features will be hard and stark; her chin will be bony, her hair more gray than black. Her clothes will be the oldest clothes I have seen on anyone, even the maasi who go to clean homes. The picture of destitution. There is a slight movement, and my glance flicks up to her. She has tightened her arms and narrowed her eyes.

"Were there girls there? I'm sure that haraam zaada Juman must have arranged for you to meet some girls. Did he get you cigarettes? Or his father's bottle to drink from?"

"It was just us, we went to the river. We didn't do anything."

Then my school bag slips off my shoulder and falls by my feet. I reach down to pick it up but my mother leaps forward and snatches it out of my hand. She pulls the zip and shakes the bag over the floor.

I hold my breath as the objects fall out: books, a pencil, a few exercise books, a ruler, a scrap of paper. What else is there? My mother puts her hand inside and pulls out a cigarette. The cigarette is from weeks ago, from an afternoon when I had tried one with Kawsar and Juman and then put the extra one in the bag, forgetting all about it.

To my mother, it is proof of everything sordid she imagines all day long. She sounds almost happy in her triumph. "You think you can hide your dirty self from me, do you? You think you are oh so big now," and here she puts her hands on her hips and sticks out her chest and pulls a grotesque face, "Mr. Big Smoker Man with a scrawny mustache."

I wrap my anger around my organs, protecting them. I remove from my mind any images from the afternoon when I had laughed with my friends, because that is a false me, and this is the real me, the person that I am inside this house, in front of this woman. But the longer she goes on speaking the thinner that protection gets until I fear that my rawness will start to be exposed. Abruptly, I run into my room. From a space behind my desk, I bring out the key I had gotten made in secret. With shaking hands, I lock the door.

From the other side, I can still hear my mother. "Have you seen your face in the mirror? You think that's a mustache? You think that *thing* above your lips makes you a full-grown man who doesn't have to follow his mother's rules anymore? You're going to be like Juman's father, sleeping with whores from the City and drinking. That's all you'll be."

There is nowhere in my room to block her sound. Just the desk with the single drawer, a small cupboard, and a narrow bed with a worn-out sheet. I pull it over my head, lying on the mattress with faded outlines of urine stains from when I was a little boy. I stay there until I hear my father come home at night.

———

When I was younger, and my father found me in bed after my mother had said or done something to send me there, he would sit for a moment by my feet and tell me, in an awkward, conciliatory way, that it wasn't my mother's fault. She was sad, and worried, and she had been sad and worried for a long time, so I had to try harder to be a good, thoughtful child. And, he would say, getting up, it was she who had chosen my name, my very special name, so that I would not see a day of discomfort in my life.

My mother named me Baadal because she thought a name which means cloud would keep all of us in cool shade and fresh water. But after me there came two sisters who died, one after the other. I don't have any memory of their faces; I was only six or seven then. There is a picture of each of them in small oval frames on a little table in the living room. In them, Gulaab is three and Kanwal is one, the oldest ages they got to live. Sometimes, after crying in her room, my mother would come out and sit next to me and start talking about how hot and thirsty everyone had been in all the years that my sisters were alive, but that the summer after Kanwal passed away, it had rained very hard. And she would ask me what kind of black magic had I practiced. I learned that the best recourse was silence; if I did not answer her, she would not cry and tear at her hair, she would not wish loudly that God had taken me instead of her angelic daughters.

I remember that rain, and a gray patch that had started to grow in a corner of the living room ceiling. My father had looked at it, smiled his half smile, and said, "That to me is not an eyesore." My mother had looked at it, sighed, and said, "What a waste, paint and plaster sucking up all that water." The rain continued and the patch became darker and larger. My mother walked around the room, pausing to look out through the window and wring her hands, passing under the wet patch and glaring at it, clicking her tongue. I remember telling her I wanted to go outside and play in the puddles, but she said I couldn't do that. It would be an unholy thing to do; wasting water was a sin. If I continued to plead she would become bigger and more dangerous so I sat in a corner and made paper boats. By late afternoon the rain grew more intense, needles of it striking the ground outside. Everything became dark with water—the roofs of houses, the leaves on the trees, the strips of soil on the sides of the street, the street itself. The gray patch began to drip. My mother put a bucket under it. She joined me at the window, and together we watched the rainwater form small puddles. I was extremely aware of her presence next to me, of her tense, bony form. She could so easily reach out a hand and grab me, I made her angry even when I did not speak. When she moved I took a step back, but she only went to the kitchen, fetched a pot and a teacup, and walked out of the house. Through the glass, I saw her squat in front of a puddle, scoop up water using the cup, and empty it into the pot, her hair coming lose from the bun, sticking to her face, her mouth moving as she talked to herself. I watched her for a few more seconds before running outside with my arms full of paper boats. "Baadal! Come here and help me!" I heard her say, but I kept running toward my friend's home, my mouth open to let the water in.

The third day of that rain, it reduced to a steady drizzle. A lady from the neighborhood came by with a small plate of halwa. She gave me a five-rupee note and said, "Bless you, son." On the fourth day my mother dragged the mattress off her bed and slept there, monitoring the bucket under the dripping ceiling. When she ran out of pots and pitchers to fill from the puddles, she came up with a system to empty them quickly and efficiently: she began washing our clothes with the rainwater. My father tried to help, but her speed and system overwhelmed him. Once, he sloshed water onto the carpet and my mother told him he was useless. She put her arm out and he stumbled. For a long time, I thought they had done a playful thing but now I know better.

Juman doesn't come to school on Tuesday but that is nothing unusual; he is a casual visitor to the classroom. During break time, a boy runs over to me and Kawsar and tells us our friend Juman is being beaten up. We forget that our bags are still inside and we have half a day of school left. We run all the way to Juman's house, the boy in the front. Men are standing in a circle, from the center of which we can hear another man's voice, screaming, and a boy's voice, laughing. The men part easily and Kawsar and I see Juman bent over with his arms over his head and his father holding him by the collar of his shirt with one hand and hitting him with the sole of a shoe with the other. He growls through gritted teeth, and Juman bursts into more giggles, though his face is wet. His father changes his grip on the shoe and brings down the heel upon Juman's back.

Kawsar and I rush forward and grab him from behind, pulling him off Juman. The men, who have been watching silently until now, start saying, in tones of reason, "Come on, end this now" and "Someone get him a glass of water." At that, I let go of Juman's father and look around for my friend. We find him a few doors down the street, surrounded by boys from the school. He is sitting on the ground. His right eye is swollen and his lip is bleeding. A bruise is blooming over his cheek. When he sees us he grins, and we see he has a tooth missing on one side. Kawsar turns his face away for a moment and passes a hand over his eyes.

"What happened with your abba?" I ask.

Juman caresses his face. "Nothing, really. That pig Mohsin told my father I broke his dish antenna, and my father broke my face."

"Did you?"

Juman's smile becomes wider. "Of course."

The teachers in our school have been in a bad mood lately because Mrs. Zeenat, the one who fainted, has gone back to the City. Our science teacher spends the lesson shaking his head and saying people like Mrs. Zeenat never completely want to belong to the Town. "How could she have," he goes on, "when every Friday her sister or brother or someone sent her a box full of her favorite snack foods?" When the volunteer history teacher comes in, he first says, "This place isn't for weaklings. It is not for soft people. It is not for greedy or needy or inward-looking people." Then he tells us to take out our pens and take notes. We write and learn. Many years ago, the people in the villages of Purana Gaon, Duur Gaon, and Naya Gaon went through a terrible trial that came to be called the Great Shrinking. Bara Darya lost a lot of volume; everything important became less—food, blind dependency on something as free-flowing as water. What increased was dread, and the number of children. People migrated toward the north and settled here in the Town, where the river was still a little stronger.

There is nothing new in this for us; the stories of how people came and settled into the Town were the words we learned to speak as babies. Just like we have been taught that almost every child born here has been given a name meant to evoke a sensation of coolness, of thirst being quenched. We are a generation of leaf, rain, sea, cool breeze. We are supposed to ward off unhappiness, and live.

The history teacher, who is from the City after all, points to us and says, in an incredulous tone, "And after all the loss they had seen their own parents go through, they didn't seem to want to stop having children. First one child, then two, then four. Birthing them and burying them, on and on and on."

I wonder if he knows that Kawsar, whose name is a river in heaven, used to have six brothers and sisters, and the youngest one died after eight days, and then a brother, and then another.

My father works in a pharmacy. It is the only one in town. He is the owner's assistant. For as long as I have known him, he has put on his light-blue striped shirt and his dark gray pants and driven off in his little car to the small, square building full of medicine. Kawsar's father smells like soil, Juman's father smells of cigarettes and alcohol. My father has no particular smell attached to him. He stays in the shadow of my mother, walking around thin and stoop-shouldered, not speaking much. He does not scold me about my studies, he does not give me lectures about life. After he comes home from work, he goes to the TV, turns it on, and does not move from in front of it until ten, when he gets up to go to bed. We eat our dinner with him in front of whatever he is watching, which is usually the news or a talk show. I like watching the ads. Like everything else on TV, they come from the City, and they are full of City accents and problems and affectations. I stop eating whenever they come on. They show a different world—perfumes, big families around long tables, cheeky grins on children's shiny faces, grandfathers who are clean and glowing with health and nobleness, nobody troubled with debilitating amounts of thirst or want, nobody writhing in pain. The distance between here and the City is only the length of a road but there might as well be a sea in the middle.

Sometimes people go there and bring back gifts. A girl in my class once started coming to school with big, shiny bows in her hair; she said her aunt got them for her from a store in the City. Sometimes people go there and never return, like Juman's uncle, who hasn't been back to the Town in more than twelve years. Married a *saali*, did not even invite his sisters to the wedding. *Saali* was a word my friends and I learned from Juman when we were little. He said his mother had used it with her jaw clenched; he imitated it, the word coming out like a hiss. We understood it must mean something bad.

My father tells us during a break in a program: Kawsar's father is going to have to close his grocery store.

"In all these years—fifteen to be exact—I have never been out of work," he continues, softly, the words going up and down like a song. "Not even when I was a young man in Purana Gaon, during that most trying of times."

"Talk about something else," my mother says.

"We have always had something to eat. Even if it was a few pieces of bread a day."

"Don't say it." My mother's voice is as hard and brittle as a twig.

"Even if it was just a cup of water. Or a potato. Or an ice cream." My father laughs. "Remember, Raheela, when that group sent us a refrigerated van full of ice cream? What a scramble that was. What a pushing and shoving. Muzaffar ran away with a whole liter tub of melting vanilla under his arm!"

"You're going to bring it back. All the bad, it's going to come back if you keep talking this way. I will not allow you to do that." My mother's eyes are wide and wet but not with tears, I am sure; she is not that type of person.

My father's sound dies and he shuts his mouth. My mother turns up the volume of the TV, and the three of us move our faces toward the man on the screen.

When I was five years old, Kawsar's uncle bought him a football from the City. We played with it for a while. I went home with dirt on the front of my shirt, on my pants, on my cheeks and hands. It was only when I saw the look on my mother's face that I realized the condition I was in. She pulled me by my arm and hauled me back outside. She bent down and gathered a handful of soil. With her other hand she held me in place as she pushed the dirt into my mouth. Before I fainted, I saw my father's face appear at the window then move away.

But my mother has been gentle too. I remember, after my first sister had died and the second one was in her belly, leaving the house with her one morning. We walked for a long time, then rode in a rickshaw for a long time. I remember her carrying me until we arrived at the high walls of a house. "We must be quiet or the uncle who lives inside will get very angry," she whispered to me. Giggling, we slipped through a pair of large gates and into a green field. I had never stepped in so much grass before. I remember her hand over my eyes and then, a word from her: "Look!" In front of us was a small pond. My mother put her feet in it and told me to do the same. She spread her dupatta on the grass, sat on it, and read out loud from a book she produced from her bag. After a while, she tied one end of the dupatta around my waist and the other around her wrist. Then she lay on the grass and covered her eyes with her arm. "Don't go too far," she said, unnecessarily because I did not want to be far from this vision of my mother on the grass with a book. While she slept, I picked up sticks and leaves.

A year ago I had looked for that house from my memory. I found a haveli at the edge of the Town. Nobody had lived in it for some time. The padlock on the gates had rusted, then been broken by someone. I went through. Instead of grass there were dried, yellow-brown sticks here and there in clumps. I couldn't find a pond but there was an area which could have once carried water. I stood where I thought my mother and I had stood. Nobody could have seen us from the house. I stayed there for some time, and when the afternoon became more blue and less yellow, I left.

ෆ

The sun is huge and fierce for almost fourteen hours a day now. Spring, however long it lasted—a few days or a few minutes—has ended. One morning on my way to school I see clouds drift into the sky and I hold my breath; maybe they will stay and become bigger and grayer and release rain. But the clouds leave.

That night, my father says, "Nobody wants to be treated anymore. It's as if everyone has decided to go without medication." Parents are trying to cure their children's fevers with onions, he goes on. A woman's husband injured his foot while digging, and she blew prayers over a cloth and tied it around his wound. A small girl told her mother at night that she could not sleep from a stomachache, and her mother sang and patted her back until, exhausted, the girl closed her eyes. The pharmacy is losing money. Then my father becomes quiet, his eyes on the TV where the weather reporter is saying there are no chances of rain in Purana Gaon, Naya Gaon, or Duur Gaon, in Araam Gaon, Beech Gaon, or Qareeb Gaon, or the Town.

A boy in my class, the son of a farmer, has stopped coming to school. His father grows a few crops on the outskirts of the Town. A friend of the boy's tells us what happened: the boy's father got hold of a bottle of sleeping pills from the pharmacy, swallowed them, and died. Later, at break time, a group of my classmates surround me. They stand with their hands curled into fists, their faces severe.

"Your father sold the pills that killed Jan's father," one of them says.

"Your father is a murderer," says another.

"No he's not!" I wonder where Kawsar is. "He didn't know Jan's father would do something like that."

"Your father is alive, helping more people die, but Jan's is dead."

"It's not my fault!"

A boy kicks my right leg. The pain travels up, reaching my groin, making me want to pee. A foot strikes my stomach. I double over and wet myself. I am pushed to the ground, my cheek pressed into gravel. After a while the boys walk away. When I can't hear their footsteps and voices anymore, I get up slowly and start walking.

A month later, the pharmacy where my father works burns to the ground. It was a deliberate act, my father tells me and my mother, looking lost and old. He describes how the owner started the fire. First, he filled two boxes with bottles and boxes and asked my father to set them outside on the ground, near the road. "Painkillers, antacids, burn ointments, and cough syrups," my father recites. "Heart medicine, decongestant, nasal sprays, eye drops. He wouldn't tell me why I had to move them out." My father sighs, and his body shakes slightly. "He locked himself inside the pharmacy. I saw him pour lighter fluid over the floor and the shelves. The walls. Then he lit a match, threw it down, and everything caught fire."

"He didn't get out?" I ask.

A small moan escapes my father's mouth.

"Where are the boxes?" my mother asks.

"I think I left them there."

"You should bring them home. There is important medicine in there."

He stands obediently, then leaves. He comes back in half an hour, enters the house with a box. My mother gets up. He takes out a bottle and throws it down. He takes out another and smashes that one too. Brown liquid and tiny pieces of glass cover the floor. My mother shouts at him to stop but he breaks another one, then another. Still screaming, she runs into her room and shuts the door. I step around my father and leave the house.

Around midnight, when I come back, I find him asleep on the sofa, and ants stuck to the outline of the syrup.

2

THE MURAL

Two times a week, a bus goes from the Town into the City. When someone wants to move out of here, they take this bus. There is a lot of interest in those who leave. People ask their relatives for updates: "How are they doing? Has Rashid (or Taha or Ahmed or whoever) found work yet? Is little Neher enjoying her new school? How many bedrooms does their new home have?" Almost every time the update is, "You know how it is over there. I've explained to Rashid to take what he can get, but he's being a bit stubborn." Here, the relative adds an indulgent, worried chuckle. "Says he's an engineer, won't settle, etc. etc. Oh, how many bedrooms? Well, right now they're in one room in some area next to a railway line, but they've got their eye on a smart little apartment." A month later we hear from the relative, "Rashid is a technician at the electric company, goes on one of those trucks all over the city if there's a problem in the lines. No, the apartment was too far, they are staying in that room for now. No, they are not coming back."

We also hear other things, such as how the City people feel about us constantly moving into their land, taking up their water, changing the shape of their place with our shacks and grubby children. We hear that Neher's parents are changing her name to Nargis because nobody in her school has a name which means little stream. Nobody in all of the big City is called anything like that.

෪

The math teacher has decided to teach us a new subject: Purana Gaon. Purana Gaon is a village only thirteen kilometers away. There is no textbook for this course. Once a week, toward the end of the lesson, our teacher puts away the math textbook and takes out a different one. This new book is from the country's tourism board, he tells us. He holds it up for all of us to see: glossy photographs of simple streets, lines of trees, sun-browned rustic faces of children and the elderly smiling wisely and shyly into the camera. He reads out lists of facts and short passages. "There is much to be discovered and admired about Purana Gaon. Fresh fruit, fresh air, a return to family values, things that today's young people are greatly deprived of."

A student raises his hand. "My uncle says there's no clean water there anymore."

The teacher, who is from the City, refers to his notebook and says, "Your uncle will be happy to know about the progress the government has made drilling wells in the village."

"That's a lie, my uncle says."

The teacher purses his lips thoughtfully, then says in the tone of a friendly advisor, "Would it really be so much worse for your people to move out of here? I mean, this Town is falling apart, isn't it? You should all just leave and go to the villages, the place of your parents' parents."

Aab, the girl Juman thinks likes him, is moving to the City. Two of her little cousins died from diarrhea and now nobody in her family wants to stay in the Town. Not her parents, uncles and aunts, not her grandmother from her father's side or her grandmother's brother. "Where will you live?" one of her friends asks her at break time. Juman stays on the fringe, within earshot.

Aab shrugs. "Maybe a flat."

Within two weeks, the girl and her family pack up their clothes and their kitchen, go to the bus depot, and leave. A few days after Aab moves away, Juman says he is feeling too sad to go to school. So we skip our classes and go to the girl's big, empty house. The main gate is locked; we climb over the wall and land on drying grass and earth. We have never been here before. We go around, peeking through windowpanes.

"I feel broken up inside," Juman says.

"You hardly knew her." Kawsar leans down and rips up a handful of half-dead weeds.

"She let me kiss her."

"Liar! When?" I try a door handle but it is locked.

"Behind Chacha Ameer's shop, one morning before school."

"Hard to believe a girl would let you kiss her. I mean, look at you. All ribs, no muscles." Kawsar snorts and ducks when Juman throws a stick at him.

"I told her I loved her and she said okay I could kiss her, she was leaving anyway."

Kawsar cups his hands with his eyes, presses his forehead against a window. His voice, when he speaks, is muffled. "My father sometimes says we should get out of here. But when he says it to Dadi she says she's never leaving, and then he says he's never leaving *her*, because she is his mother and he could never leave his mother."

"Does *your* mother want to move?" I ask.

"I don't know. She doesn't speak about it."

"I am definitely going," Juman says. "As soon as school is finished. Print out my CV, get a good job in the City, leave this garbage life behind. Become manager, drive my own car. A Pajero."

"A CV. What will you put in it: I touched a girl?" I laugh.

"Shut up. Better than what you'll write in yours: I have wet dreams."

I shove Juman and he stumbles.

"I'm ahead of you, friend," he says. "Saving good money from my work at that clothes shop."

Kawsar wets his finger with his spit and rubs away dust from a pane of glass. "My brother caught a cricket the other day and ate it."

"I've never eaten a cricket."

That night for dinner my mother makes an oily saalan of onions and beans. For many days after that we eat weak onion saalan flavored with salt and red chili powder. I wonder when my father will get another job. He doesn't seem to want to. My mother has made him go out every day since the pharmacy burned down. My father sprinkles talcum powder on the sweat stains in the armpits of his thin, old shirt, brushes his hair with a wet comb, and sets off on foot. Then he comes back by late afternoon, takes off his shoes, changes into his old shalwar qameez, and turns on the news. As the days go by, the food in my house appears stranger and stranger. Tiny, dark brown particles stuck to potato skins or onion peelings mixed with oil and flour. I chew it slowly and taste wood. When I go to bed, it is on a stomach that has an uncomfortable fullness to it, and aches. I wonder if Kawsar's brother was surprised when he bit into that cricket.

But we continue to grow, the girls and boys in my school. Maybe our bones have adapted quickly to sand and wood, maybe our stomachs have shrunk to the sizes of our thumbs. My school pants stop above my ankles. I don't feel too embarrassed, though, because I see that Kawsar's pants are too big for him. Almost all the girls in my class seem to fill out their old uniforms. I want to see how tight they are but the girls have started wrapping their dupattas around themselves. Sitting at the back of the class, heavy-headed and too warm, I slide into daydreams.

We get a new Urdu teacher. She is fresh from the City, therefore excited and optimistic. She asks us to analyze a poem about forbearance. She asks us to write an essay on the virtue of abstaining from too much food and water. We read a story about a learned man from centuries ago who spent two days on this bit of land that is our Town and declared it was a blessed land, a place for special people. She brings her TV and VCR to school in her car all the way from her home and for the next five days we watch short videos on the topics of true happiness in the face of trials. Then, one afternoon, the fans in the classroom stop moving; the power has gone out. We find it harder and harder to move our pens over paper and our eyeballs over text. We become hot and thirsty. We become tired of studying the same subject. One by one we fall asleep, or maybe only I do.

My mother has started making loud sounds at home. She sighs and moans as she dusts; when she is in the kitchen, she mutters. She walks slowly and holds her hips though she is not an old woman. My father keeps his eyes down or in front of him, never straight at her, not even when she is addressing him. The color of his face does not change, the slow movements of his jaws as he chews remain the same. I stay out later and later but no matter what time I come home my mother is there, waiting for me with the light turned off. She yells out words as I rush to my room. Liar, thief, shit thief, bastard liar. I stop going home after school. I go to Chacha Ameer's shop where, once every few days, I manage to convince him to give me an old packet of chips.

I meet my friends at Darya Park one day, after Juman is done at the clothes shop. There was a poster with a photograph of this park in the pharmacy that was set on fire. In the picture, the trees were a bright green, the sky a wonderful blue, the grass laid out like a carpet. The park we go to contains the same three things—grass, trees, sky—but they are all shades of yellow. It is how my friends and I have always known it. Only the water in the stream has changed a little in front of us. It has gone down by a few inches, revealing mud clinging to rocks. We take off our shoes, roll up the legs of our pants, and go down the short slope. The mixture of soil and water comes up to a little above our ankles. We curl and uncurl our toes and drag our feet through the ooze. Kawsar begins to walk toward a small puddle in the drying stream. He pulls his T-shirt over his head and flings it onto the bank on our right. When he reaches the puddle, he gets down on his hands and knees and lies down in the water, face to one side.

"Have you gone crazy?" Juman laughs.

"Get up, you look stupid," I say.

Kawsar raises himself on one elbow, scoops water with one hand into his mouth.

"You'll get sick."

"Try it. It's not that bad." Kawsar's grin shows through the mud on his face.

Juman tenses up. Then he tears off his shirt and, with a wild laugh, jumps into the puddle. "Come on, Baadal!" he shouts.

It has been three weeks since my mother has allowed me to take a bath. Slowly, I kneel next to my friends. The coolness of the water spreads over and into my clothes, across my stomach and chest and down my legs. I touch the water with my tongue; the mud is gritty, like I remember it.

I get home a little after midnight. My mother is not there. I enter my room, switch on the light, and see my schoolbooks on the floor, torn in half along their spines. I lock my door. From my bag, I pull out other books, the ones she missed, and, one by one, render them into halves of themselves. It is easy; they are all old, used several times over, the paper giving way easily. I turn out the light and lay on my bed, digging my fingernails into my arms until I fall asleep.

My father has got a job. This is how he tells us he found it: "I went to a shoe seller, I sat on the floor, and I cried. The shoe seller said, you can help me with my accounts. And I said, thank you."

He brings us two pairs of shoes from the shop, one for my mother and one for me. They are imperfect; one pair has faulty soles and the other has misaligned shoelace holes. That's why he was able to get them for a lot less than their original price. I give Kawsar my old shoes and he puts them on without any questions, throwing away his own broken ones whose soles had begun to flap when he walked. He is very careful with his new shoes; whenever we are in the shade, he takes them off and walks barefoot.

Our school principal told us today that we have received funding from the City for a special Town project: everyone from class 10 and above has to participate in the creation of a mural. We are to paint the wall across from the school, on the other side of the main road. The principal read from a paper in his hand. "You are to make pictures of butterflies, rainbows, trees, ponds, fish in ponds. Happy things."

The main road is wide but crossing it is easy because there are not many cars at this time of the morning. We carry buckets of paint and a large brush each. Our teacher makes groups of us and tells us what to do. "You paint pink flowers, the size of your palms. You make a tree; make sure the trunk is brown and the leaves are green." He hands each group a piece of paper with a picture on it. The teacher moves down the line to where Juman, Kawsar, and I are waiting. "You have to paint a stream that will flow along the last third of the wall, all the way from one end to the other." In addition to a sheet of paper, he gives us two trays. "For when you need to mix." He moves on and I hear him say, from group to group, "Fish. Spray of water. Green grass."

We look at the paper in my hands. It has a single photograph of a wide stream, with flecks of white mixed up with gray. It looks like a living body of water, nothing like the sluggish one in Darya Park. Juman whistles and says, "This isn't an intestine."

"Do we have enough for all that?" Kawsar asks. We examine the cans of paint given to us; dark blue, black, white. They seem very measured and precise and well thought-out. Hesitantly, we dip our brushes into the colors and move the bristles over the wall. After a few minutes Juman empties a little blue and a little white on one of the trays. We spend all morning painting the stream. When the teacher tells us that we are done we rise stiffly, surprised by how sweaty our faces and how cramped our fingers are.

We paint for three days in a row. We go to school, we leave our bags in our classrooms, we cross the road and make our stream, our controlled sunshine, our imaginary beasts and healthy cows, our insects and plants. On the fourth day we start to settle down by the wall when the teacher on duty starts to shout. "Kasrat! Kasrat!" I look up to see a boy standing in the middle of the road. *What is he waiting for?* I wonder dully, my mind busy on getting the correct combination of colors to get a nice gray for a section of the stream. Kasrat doesn't look back at us. The teacher starts to walk toward him at the same time that a van appears around a corner and comes down the road. The teacher is now running; the van swerves into another lane but Kasrat is fast; he gets his legs struck. We are sent home early.

Two days later we resume painting the mural. News flows up and down the line: Kasrat has fractures in both legs; what he really wanted to do was die; he was tired of being hot and hungry. His parents are trying to arrange a transfer to a City hospital. They really should have been careful when naming him Kasrat, which means abundance.

By the end of the month we finish the mural. It is colorful and busy. We admire each other's skills and shyly admit that our own work isn't too bad. The school principal takes photographs of the wall and of us with a camera lent to him by the same group that has funded this whole project.

"They will put it in the City's newspaper," he tells us.

Kawsar tells me he had a vision a few days ago. In his vision he saw a white shirt with crisscrossing black stripes on the front and back. He says the shirt is at the used clothes shop and he is going to go get it, he's got enough money for it. I look at Kawsar's triangular face and his eyes which appear overlarge in it. We go to the shop together. It is the same one where Juman is working. I don't see him there but there are too many other things inside to think about that. The shop is a room with three tables in the middle and a few shelves along the walls. On one table there is a jumble of T-shirts, pants, and shalwar qameez. This is the men's section. Next to it is ladies' clothing; more colorful, longer. The shelves have more items, boxes with labels written on them in black marker: CHILD 2–4, or CHILD/BOY 6–8, etc. Some say SHOES. One box reads TIES/SHOELACES. Kawsar is already busy holding T-shirts up in the fluorescent light. They are white with blue stripes.

"Is that the one you saw?" I ask.

"No, the stripes are wrong."

I leave him to his hunt and hold up a jacket. When I see a shirt similar to the one Kawsar thinks he had a vision of, I pick it up for him to see. I am trying on a pair of blue shoes when I hear him shout, "I found it!" He is holding a black shirt with the pattern he described.

"That is some luck," I say. From the corner of my eye I see the store clerk raise his head from behind his table.

Kawsar holds the creased shirt carefully. "I knew I would find it."

"I'm happy for you, friend."

He smiles brightly and goes to pay.

Kawsar wears that shirt every day, even on the hottest days. I try to stay at home for dinner so I can save some part of it to take to him. Weeks go by and he doesn't mention another vision, so I think his mind has stopped going away because there is a little more food in his body. But one day he says to me and Juman that behind the tire shop is a rusting tin box, and in the box is a puppy, and we follow him in his graying white shirt with the black stripes to where the tires make a rubber labyrinth, and when he rushes ahead then falls into a crouch, we run to him and find him holding a puppy.

∾

In July everything in the Town settles into an uneasy stillness. Brown houses sit heavily upon the earth. People walk slower, conserving energy. When we walk, our shirts quickly become dark with our sweat. We stay silent; if we open our mouths they become filled with wool-like thirst. Then, in two days, two children die of dysentery, and these were children of people who live in the bigger houses with painted bricks, so news of their deaths goes around the Town very quickly. Other things we hear: the father from one set of the parents screams at the doctor for killing his child. Then he walks into the school and bellows at the child's teacher. The teacher does not fight back, does not wipe away the father's spittle that has landed on his face. When the father is done, the teacher quietly hands him the child's half-full water bottle. At home the father empties all of it into his mouth and hugs it as he curls up in bed. He falls sick, refuses treatment, and dies.

The principal shuts down the school, walks to the river in the park, and settles down on a bedsheet with prayer beads in one hand. His wife waits until nightfall for him to come back home, and when he doesn't, she goes down to talk to him. He tells her he is going to stay by the river for a while, maybe a week or a month. His wife said she doesn't understand, and why is he not wearing his nicer clothes? Why is he in a shirt with a torn collar and pants with holes in the knees? He explains to her gently that there has been so much death in the Town because people are not being honest with themselves about their sins. His wife loses the color in her face, looks at her husband, wide-eyed, and croaks, "You have gone crazy." She goes away, angry and crying. Our principal stays on his bedsheet.

People start visiting him. Some think he looks more translucent and pure; others, like his wife, think he ought to be forcefully carried home. Those who believe in him become a larger group than those who don't. I join them one day.

"This is a bad time again," he says to us, raising his voice a little. It is thin, like his hair, which now touches his earlobes.

Some in the crowd moan and shake their heads in agreement.

"This is because among us all we have accumulated a lot of wrong. A great deal of wrong. Until that is properly atoned for, we are not going to have water from above or below."

"That is the truth!" someone yells.

"We must give up lying."

"We must stop lying," the people echo.

"And cheating."

"No cheating."

"And stealing."

"No more!"

"And lusting."

"Never."

"We need to do some purification," the principal says. "And that can only be done if we spend some time by the river, reflecting, away from our usual habits of wanting, always wanting."

The tire shop owner shuts down his failing business and sets up camp by the river. Then a grandmother leaves her son's house and joins him; she tells her family to give away her bed. Two sisters walk out of their tin-roofed shack while their aunt tries to follow them up the street, throwing pebbles at them and yelling for them to come back. In another part of Town, a man waits for his brother to leave the house for a smoke and a drink, then locks the door. When the brother hammers on the door, the man tells him he'll only let him back if he cures himself by the water. Juman says to us, with a laugh, that he wishes his father would walk all the way into the river and drown.

I find out that my mother also has ideas about who should go there. One evening, she says to no one in particular, "That woman Meena means to cause trouble. She has no reason to go on staying in that house, trapping strange men. She should pack up her bags and live in the park like those other crazy people."

I ask, "Who is Meena?"

She ignores me and turns to my father. "What do you think?"

My father says, "There is a new drama on TV."

Once a week at ten, we watch *Bara Shehr, Baray Khwaab. Big City, Big Dreams*, in fat, curvy letters below the Urdu title. It is about a girl and her family. She looks around sixteen or seventeen. She has brown hair and wears jeans with a long shirt. She is nothing like me. She is nothing like the people around me. For the next six weeks, in twenty-minute episodes, I watch her and her family. I fall in love with all of them: the father with his short, black hair, the mother who wears pink and yellow shirts, the little sister who is a mini version of the older one with braided hair, their big, tall brother. I memorize their accents, their slang words, their mannerisms. I inhale their wholesomeness. One afternoon, while walking around the Town, Juman says something the brother in the show had said. He does the City accent really well. Kawsar responds as if he is the father. I pretend to be the older sister. It doesn't seem important who we are playing. What matters is that for a few moments we become different people.

I ask my friends about Meena. Kawsar says he heard that her husband left her some time ago for another woman in the City, started a whole new family.

"Maybe he got sick of her," Juman says. "Maybe she screamed at him or hit him or something. Maybe she turned ugly."

"She's not ugly. She came to our house once. Asked my mother for some work, said she'll clean floors and cook and everything."

"What's her face like?" Juman asks.

"She's not like the girls in our school, you know; she's much older. Like an aunt or something."

"Yes, but is she beautiful?"

Kawsar shrugs. "She's not ugly."

"Did your mother give her the job?" I ask.

"No. She said my father wouldn't allow it. But she gave her some money and clothes."

Juman thinks the three of us should go to the City. He says he's tired of the stream and the sad, empty houses and the sad, empty faces around him. He wouldn't mind setting fire to all of it.

"No car," I say.

Juman clicks his tongue in impatience. "We could borrow from someone."

"Nobody would lend it to us."

But one morning he is outside the school, and when Kawsar and I arrive he grabs us by the straps of our bags and quickly steers us away from the gate. "What the hell's going on?" I ask, and Juman lets go and begins to run. "Hurry!" he cries. So we pick up our feet and follow him, bags thumping on our backs. He disappears inside a narrow street. When we get there, we see him standing beside a white sedan. Juman grins and gets in on the driver's side. Kawsar and I open doors and scramble onto the seats.

"Whose car is this?" Kawsar's voice comes out high pitched.

Juman starts the engine and fiddles with the radio.

I remember now. "Hold on, isn't this Aab's uncle's car, the one with the limp? He let you take his car? Wasn't he coming back for it from the City?"

"Shut up," Juman says. "He doesn't know. He's not even here."

"I'm not sitting in a stolen car," says Kawsar.

"It's only for today, you idiot. Just to the City and back, okay? I'll refill the petrol as well, happy?"

Juman grips the steering wheel with both hands and hunches over it. A woman on the radio speaks excitedly about the weather and the traffic, then a song starts. I've heard it played at the barber's. It's a good tune. From the backseat, I see Kawsar move his head along to it. In a little while we arrive at the road that goes out of the Town. We sit straighter, fix our hair with our hands. Juman changes the radio station; the song playing on this one was very popular last month. It came on almost every evening before the news. Kawsar tries to say the words but he gets them wrong.

The part of the City we enter looks nothing like the shows on TV, but we don't care. All that matters is that there is an excess of everything in this place that none of us have been in before. Juman drives past shops, people, fruit, hand-cranked juicing machines on carts. We have left behind thirst and thinness, the sense of depletion. Juman has money, he buys us a bun kebab each. We are hungrier after it. He buys us three more. We don't ask him where he got the money from. We turn a corner and find ourselves on a wide, quiet road with trees on both sides. Small yellow flowers hang in heavy bunches among the green leaves. We drive in silence past large houses fronted with spiked gates and guards. I think we are relieved when, once again, we reach a busy area filled with shops. Juman parks parallel to a shoe store.

"I need some things from in there," he says.

"Those are good," Kawsar says, pointing at the shop's window.

I look at the shoes: black all over, thick white soles, orange laces. To our right, Juman goes in and we follow. There is no shopkeeper. We call out a few times and go to the back to see if there is another room but find nothing and no one. Juman grins and pulls down a pair of joggers. Kawsar steps outside while I stand in the middle of the floor, not sure if I should stop Juman or let him be. Kawsar comes back. "The man has gone for prayers. They say he will be back in half an hour."

"You are an idiot for asking," Juman says, but he is too delighted with what he has on his feet to be truly angry or worried. He marches over to the window and brings down the black shoes. He throws them over to Kawsar. Then he points at my feet and says, "Come on, you know you don't want to look like a poor Town beggar."

We run to the car with different shoes on our feet, in our arms, strung around our necks with the laces tied, feeling happy and strong with our haul. The roads have become fuller in the time we were inside the shop; all around us, children are going home. The traffic moves slowly and Juman stays behind a van, stopping when it stops, moving again when it moves, until it parks by a school. Juman also parks. The school gate is open and older boys and girls are walking out.

Kawsar peers at the sign above the building. "Grammar School, Senior Campus."

"Let's go talk to them," Juman says, pointing at a small group of girls standing by the wall.

"What? Why?"

"Why not?"

"Because we're from the *Town*?" I say.

Juman makes an impatient sound. "What does it matter where we're from?" He puts his hand on the door and Kawsar grabs his shirt.

"Okay, but don't call me Kawsar in front of them."

Juman shakes off his hand. "Fine! I'll call you Babar, like the king, is that better? And I'll be Ahmed and Baadal is Taimur. Okay?"

He steps out of the car first, and we follow slowly. My mouth is dry and my stomach is feeling unsettled but my feet feel good in my new shoes. As we walk toward the girls, I try to remember if my plain white school shirt has any old stains on it. I try to smile a little but it feels unnatural. I wonder what we'll do if the girls' parents appear. And then we are right in front of them and Juman is introducing us. He has forgotten my given name, making it Tariq instead of Taimur, but that's okay, the girls are smiling. The one with her hair in a smooth ponytail asks us which school we go to and I find myself making a joke, not giving a direct answer. The words come easily to me. Even the way I'm standing, with my hands casually in my pockets, feels natural. We stand outside that school talking with the girls for almost ten minutes when the tallest one says, "You're from the Town, aren't you?"

Kawsar answers, "Yes."

I think, *It's all right, it doesn't matter.*

The girl says, "My cousin's aunt collected clothes for the people there once." The girl still sounds friendly. But she is interested in us in a different way now. The three of us have collectively altered, diminished.

"My car is here, it was nice meeting you," one of the girls says. I don't know which one, and it does not matter.

After this we don't feel like doing much else. We drive back home. After a few minutes, Kawsar asks, "How did they know?" And I tell him, because suddenly I understand, "Our school pants are shit brown." We become silent again, listening to the low-volume drone coming from the radio.

Ↄↄ

Juman gets busy, writing his CV and trying to find a place he can get it typed and printed. The hospital in the Town hires Kawsar as a cleaner and part-time receptionist.

"Why don't you find something too?" he says. This irritates me because I know I must do something; I must have a plan. I am done with school and school is done with me, I have no reason to behave as if I am still a fifteen-year-old boy.

"Maybe you could get a vision and tell me what it is I am supposed to do." I laugh as if I am making a joke, but I know my words are cruel. I don't try to stop Kawsar as he walks away.

My mother sees my face at home and the muscles of her features change and her eyes become small and her nostrils widen and her mouth moves. She does other things too: she sets a plate in front of my father and none in front of me. She drags a chair to the door of the living room and sits on it. My father stares at his food and she shouts, "Eat it! Now." Then she points a finger at me and in a dangerously sweet voice, says, "You. You sit down there, amazing son of mine, too good to work." She crosses her arms. "Eat your dinner," she commands my father again, and he picks up a tiny morsel and puts it in his mouth. When he gets up and tries to feed her, she begins to cry, and I escape.

But she is not done. In the week after that she starts following me, speaking increasingly garbled words: "What time would you like your dinner, baadshah, your Noble Excellency? Can't you see that your father is getting old, getting paid more in old shoes and less in money?" I run out and she is behind me. "Your Royal Heap of Cow Manure, Your Fancy Lordship," she says in a mimicking voice.

"Stop it!" I scream. I tear a pile of newspapers. I throw a glass plate on the floor and it shatters. I turn toward the door, pushing past my mother, past my father, who is sitting in front of the screen, eyebags and mouth sagging, pretending he cannot hear a thing.

3

MIRACLES

THERE IS REPORT OF A MIRACLE around the end of August. It is by a pair of sisters who had gone away to the river together but set up their living areas four feet away from each other. They return to their homes and tell their husbands that from the fourth day to the sixth one, their last day, the grass around them had been green and springy. Their brother goes to check but comes back saying his sisters were lying, the grass over that whole area is burnt yellow and pale brown. The women are reprimanded for spreading false news, but they only shrug and say they saw what they saw, and they have nothing to gain from lying. Then a few days later, a man returns from the river and says that he met a talking fish. He sends his daughter-in-law to corroborate his story. She spends three days addressing the water and in the end reports that she couldn't see a single fish there. "But," she quickly adds. "There was a special feeling in the air. I don't know how to describe it."

After this, narrations about miracles increase. A cloud that never moved, a cool breeze which blew only over and around the secluded ones, a bird that dropped berries over a certain person. These people, when they return, say they feel forgiven and renewed and that they will never fall into sin again. But I don't think their special feelings last for long. I see a few of them as they go about the Town. They look thinner and leatherier than before they had gone. One of them had to bury her little son recently and her mouth was puckered and her hair was white as she stood outside the gate of her house. When someone held out a chair for her she pushed away their hand.

"She should have taken her child to a hospital in the City instead of camping by the river," I say to my friends later.

"And who would have taken them?" Kawsar asks. "And where would have they stayed?"

He probably believes that these miracles really did happen, and that more will occur to the truly good people in the process, and that they will be a sign that soon the weather will change, crops will grow, and bellies will be full again.

But in my family, my mother wails that we have been cursed. The owner of the shoe shop where my father works has decided to go away for a week of deep thinking. He has lived a long life, he tells my father, and there are some things he has done that he is not proud of. Maybe that is what is holding back the rain from the skies. He gives my father the key to the shop and goes away. My father feels grander because of his increased responsibility. He goes earlier to the store. A couple of days later I pass by him in the afternoon and he is not asleep; instead, he is sitting near the front where he has taped a handwritten sign that says, "Shoes for every occasion! School! Wedding! Office! Home!" The window looks clean; he must have dusted it. When the owner comes back my father has no new sales to report to him. But the owner has a piece of news for my father: he is going to shut down his shop entirely and become a caretaker of the graveyard. "This line of work is hollow," the man says, indicating the shelves of shoes. "It appeals to vanity. Perhaps that is the reason we haven't made any money." My father refuses to change out of his *banyan* and shalwar, or to shave. The collection of gray, straggly hair on his face increases.

For a while, my mother goes into a frenzy of kindness, maybe in an effort to counter the effects of the baddua she believes we are under. To an old widow she takes a bedsheet, a sprig of plastic flowers I had never seen before, an egg, and two chilis in some oil. She makes a small cake out of a pinch of sugar and rice and gives it to a man on crutches whose nephew has gone to the river. She cleans up a blind woman's house with a jhaaroo and a rag. In the kitchen at home she makes me stand by her with a measuring tape while she makes four little hills of flour with a tablespoon on the stone ledge next to the stove. She says to me, "Baadal, measure how wide these are. I want to make sure each roti comes out the same size." One of the mounds of flour is an eighth of an inch wider than the rest. My mother shakes her head in impatience and mutters, "That won't do at all."

I do not feel wary of her physically anymore, and I think, *Maybe she sees me differently now.* I tell her I have to go. She looks up and there is surprise on her face, in the gray strand hanging by the side of her face, in the scratched frames of her glasses, in her faded, wrinkled qameez. "I need you to stay," she says. Then she starts again, mixing up the flour, leveling it flatter on the spoon, pouring it out into smaller mounds, making me measure.

When a man from the government arrives, the people by the river believe that another miracle has taken place. Junaid Ghani moves into Town the day I notice the coppery brownness of my urine. His official title is Liaisons Officer for Charitable Operations. Chacha Ameer says the man has taken the guest rooms on the second floor of the town's government building. The other fact that becomes known about him is that he has a brown Toyota Corolla. Within a few days of his coming into our world, there is increased movement in the neighborhood of the building he is living in. A boy who used to go my school says a large order was delivered to that place recently; there were fruits and vegetables, and even three chickens. The boy didn't know where all this had come from.

Kawsar, on a day when he gets off early from work, tells us the men had been around to the hospital. "They went into all the rooms," he says. "There was a photographer too."

"All a show for the public back in the City," Juman says.

Kawsar grins. "They gave us a carton of chikoo and another of fruit juices. I couldn't care less about their pure and honest intentions."

"I hate chikoo."

The name of a road changes. On the large, white stone rectangle that used to say Aabshaar Road are the words Shaar Road, the letters that mean water painted over. And then my father's life alters a little a few days later, when someone rings our doorbell at eight o'clock. Standing outside is a man I do not recognize. He tells me his name and I tell it to my father. He rises from the worn-out, dented hollow on the sofa. He shuffles in his slippers toward the door, shoulders hunched forward, head sticking out from the end of his thin neck, as if he is still watching TV. In the warm night air, my father and the visitor murmur words I cannot understand. Minutes go by. On the TV a man in a rainbow wig barks like a dog. The old smell of beans spreads throughout the house.

The door opens. It is my father, looking into the house, holding a shovel. "My friend and I are going to dig new wells," he says, and leaves. My mother announces that dinner is ready, but only I hear it.

This becomes our new routine: we eat, then the man comes to the door, my father puts on his shoes, collects his shovel from where it leans against the house outside, and leaves with his new friend. His absence rearranges our lives in small, definite ways: the old, dark brown oil in the chipped bowl in the kitchen smells stronger, the dust on the clock thickens, the cracks in the soles of my mother's feet begin to darken from dirt. Only one time my mother leaves the house soon after my father does. Almost two hours go by before she comes back; there are streaks of soil on her face and on the front of her qameez. Her hair is made even more fiercely into a bun, not a strand of it loose. She does not clean up the kitchen that night. And though I hear a sob and her stifling of it, and though the rays of her anger radiate from her and find me and prod me, I do not go talk to her. The next morning, the mud is gone from her clothes, my father is back, and there is the usual minor talk. And at night, the doorbell, the picking up of the shovel, and his departure once again.

I stay in my room, unwilling to spend time with my suddenly in-dustrious friends. I look through a magazine with pictures of women. I had bought it from a boy who found a bunch of them in a heap of trash while looking for food. This is how luck favored him. Juman tried to buy the whole lot but the boy refused. The inside of my mag-azine isn't as good as the cover suggests; there aren't enough pictures, only pages of long, boring articles. In other parts of the house, my mother opens and shuts cupboard doors. She does this nightly now. On my lap, I stare at a woman in her underwear. My mother walks out of her room and goes into the kitchen. She bangs pots and pans onto the floor next to the big container of sand. She begins scouring them, the rasp of grains scraping the metal. Then there is silence; my hand stays arrested over the page. The sound begins again, and I turn to another photo. After a few nights of this I, too, begin to leave. My mother tries to stop me by complaining about her aches. I comb my hair and she says her head hurts. I tie my shoelaces and she says her left eye is losing sight. I shut the door behind me as she shouts that her tooth throbs, that all her teeth throb.

My friends are easy to find; they are listening to songs on the radio outside the barber's stall. I give out the cigarettes I took from Chacha Ameer's pack last week when he was asleep. Kawsar splits a piece of bubblegum into three. Juman shows us a box with five eggs inside.

"What the hell is that?" Kawsar peers in and wrinkles his nose.

"They're old," Juman says. "We're going to throw them at that new officer Junaid Ghani's house."

"Really? These eggs can't be used at all?" I ask.

"What, your ma didn't feed you dinner today, little boy? I'm telling you these are old."

The walls of the government building within which Junaid Ghani sleeps are not easy to reach; they stand within another wall that goes all the way around.

"We can climb this, no big deal," Juman says.

So we make footholds of the imperfections in the brickwork, scale the outer wall, and drop onto soft mud on the other side. Quickly, Juman approaches the two-story house-office and throws first one egg, then another. Kawsar and I throw one each. The eggs hit the white paint with a gentle crack, turning into liquid and shell pieces. Kawsar clutches the last egg in his hand but then holds it to his chest. "I'm taking this home," he whispers. "No problem, friend," Juman says. We turn around and run, biting our lips to stifle our laughter.

I begin to walk up and down the river most days, staying away from where there are people. It is easy to avoid them. Signs of their presence are everywhere: shirts draped over bushes, sheets on the dry earth, sheets nailed to trunks of trees to create rooms. I reach an unpopulated area where the water is so low it only moves when a strong wind blows over it.

I am sitting there in a stupor one afternoon when I realize someone is walking over. I think, *It's Juman; maybe he's got the car again.* But it's a woman with her head and face covered with a black shawl. She has a canister in each hand and one under her arm. She sees me but does not stop. When she is by the river she squats down and, one by one, drags the canisters through the water. She tightens their lids on them and tries to walk back up the bank with the now-heavy canisters, but it is almost impossible for her to keep the one under her arm in place. The end of her shawl comes untucked. Her face is narrow and her mouth long, making her eyebrows seem like the largest feature. She clicks her teeth and sets down her load to fix the shawl.

I get up off the ground. "I can carry that for you." I expect her to ignore me but she says, "Okay."

I pick up the canisters. My palms are sweaty. "These are heavy."

"I would have managed. My home isn't far."

She walks ahead of me, long strides over the ground, the shawl billowing slightly in the breeze her movement creates. We are silent all the way. We go along side streets, never a main road. Fifteen minutes later she says, "The brown gate on the right is mine." She says thank you to me and tells me her name is Mrs. Meena Sarwar.

That whole week I think about her. I try to guess when she would next need to get water and wait in front of her gate, perspiring. I don't want to ring the bell. There is no movement in the street; under the heat of the sun I feel as if I am the only person in the whole Town. My head swims a little. My breakfast was a cup of weak tea and a biscuit at Chacha Ameer's shop. But I keep standing there. I want to see Meena again, and I want her to see me. I want her to talk to me, find out about me, to ask me if I am all right. I lean against the wall and close my eyes for a moment. And then there is the sound of a latch being drawn away, the squeak of a metal door.

"What are you doing here?" she asks, not angrily.

"I wanted to help you with the water."

Slowly, she hands me a canister.

4

EXCHANGES

"I HAVE BEEN TO YOUR HOUSE," Meena tells me. It is afternoon and we are walking back through Darya Park. I have a bag on my back to carry one extra water canister for her.

"When?"

"A few months ago. Before I met you. I was looking for work."

"What did my mother say?"

"She said I should go to my husband, bring him back."

There is a tight feeling in my stomach. "Are you going to?"

"It is up to him."

I do not want to talk to her after that. Perhaps she senses my mood because she doesn't say anything either. We reach her house in silence, and she says thank you, a little formally. I don't even wait to reach the end of her street before taking out of my pocket what I had originally kept for her, a little piece of chikki. I nibble at the peanut brittle, and, when it is finished, I do not feel better.

Kawsar thinks it is extremely foolish of me to go around the Town, acting like Meena's little errand boy. He also insists on calling her Miss Meena. Juman has a more philosophical view of the situation; he thinks it is just one of the many ways the people in the Town are slowly going crazy, like our school principal, or that woman who killed all her children last month.

"Or your father," Kawsar says.

"No, he's always been crazy."

I don't add my opinion because my friends do not understand. I don't think I am Meena's helper or servant. She and I talk. She wants to know about me. My friends, my family, my school. I know she comes from a place far away from the Town and that her husband still sends her cash; he sends it with a man. But sometimes the man doesn't turn up, and sometimes there is less money. "Look how little he gave this time," she says one day as the shopkeeper puts two eggs, a half-packet of bread, a small bottle of cooking oil, and a jar of apple jam into a bag. The man tells her the total. Meena rubs her thumb over the label on the jam and puts it back.

At home, my mother calls from her bedroom and asks me where I have been. I do not answer her. I shut my door and fall down on my bed. In her husband's house, Meena is eating bread and eggs bought from her husband's money; he is sheltering her and feeding her; he is there even though his body is far away. Before she turned into her street, Meena had tried to give me some of her food. But I said no, of course. I have never accepted her offers.

I sit up and look around my room; there could be something I could sell so I could buy her that jar of jam. But my shirts are so worn out I can see my skin through them if I stand in the sun, and nobody will buy my schoolbooks. I don't own a watch; I never had a rich uncle buy me one. Quietly, I walk into the living room. There is the pair of photos of my sisters, framed by trellises carved into small circles of wood. The pictures come out easily. For a moment, I want to hide them from my mother, but she might die of sadness if she thinks her daughters' images have also disappeared. I put the photos back on the table and wrap the frames in a T-shirt.

From the kitchen, I put a knife in my pocket. I return to the grocery shop and ask the man if he would take the frames in exchange for the apple jam. He peers at them closely, looks up, and says, "No." I go to other places but none of them have jam or anything else which is sweet. Even Chacha Ameer says he cannot help me though he says it regretfully, unlike the others. By late evening, I am back at the first store. My shirt is sticking to the hollow shape of my stomach and the soles of my feet are sore. I look at the man sitting on his chair by the cash register. He gives me a slow smile, fat lips baring yellowing teeth.

"Give me the jam," I say.

"It is not for free, boy."

I take the knife out of my pocket.

The man's face turns pale. "What are you doing?" he whimpers.

"Take these frames and give me the goddamn bottle."

Keeping his eyes on me, he fetches the apple jam, sets it on the counter, and jumps back. "You can keep the frames, it is okay, it is free."

He cowers and his face is wet, and that makes me growl. "You don't understand. These fucking frames are *payment*. Do you get it now?"

"Yes, sorry, thank you."

Meena is surprised and touched when I bring her the bottle. I want to hear her say, "Why don't you come in and we can eat dinner together?" She doesn't, of course, but when I see her next she gives me a sandwich with a thick layer of jam inside.

My afternoons are now spent with her, or with Juman or Kawsar, if they are free. When at home my mother will sometimes go days without speaking to me, and other times she'll rage outside my locked door, well into the early hours of the morning, calling Meena names, threatening to disown me, to set me on fire while I sleep. All of this is bearable because I have Meena. I use the money her husband sends to buy her food; I repair a broken screen in a window inside her house while she stands outside the gate and waits for me to finish; I find her medicine when she has a headache. I get lulled into thinking this is all right, this is good.

Then, on a day when nothing else seems different, I knock on Meena's door and a woman I have never seen before answers.

"What do you want, boy?" she asks.

"Nothing," I stammer. "I brought Miss Meena her grocery."

She looks at the plastic bag in my hand, takes it from me quickly as if I am diseased, and shuts the gate.

The woman stays for four days. I learn from others in the Town that she is Meena's ex-husband's oldest sister from the City. The day of her departure, a group of children gather around her as she tries to get into the van. They want sweets or money or both. She gives them nothing, telling them to get out of her way. They only scatter when the driver, the uncle of one of the children, takes a threatening step toward them.

"How did she know you were sick?" I ask Meena later in Darya Park. We are sitting at the bank of the river. She offers her hand. I refuse to take it.

"I asked her to come," she says, slowly putting her hand in her lap.

"Why?"

"I needed someone to look after me. A woman."

I shrug, wanting to hold onto my anger.

"I don't know anyone here," she adds.

"I didn't like her."

"She's okay." Then Meena gives a short laugh. "She wants me and him to get back together. She says he is very unhappy. He was under the influence of a very cunning witch for a very long time and he is getting better now."

I don't see how she can sound happy, as if all this is a joke, a lighthearted matter.

I say, "But you can't believe that bullshit. He left you."

"Back then either one of us could have left. He just did it first."

I feel submerged; I don't understand any of this.

"Are you going to the City?" I ask her. "Do you want to get back with him?"

"No."

But I don't feel comforted. In the distance, a man gets up and begins walking with slow steps. I had not noticed him before. He stumbles, kneels on the ground, and turns his face toward me. I quickly look away. I have always tried to keep my eyes on the ground when passing by the campers so that I do not accidentally recognize anyone in a moment when they might be repenting or praying. Once at home I had walked in on my mother when she was bent over the floor, crying and complaining to no one I could see, and it was a disturbing sight. From the corner of my eye I see the man get up and wave. At that moment, I feel hatred toward him and all others like him, soiling the air with the smells of their bodies and with their feces buried under soil. I hate myself the most for not being able to keep Meena to myself.

Meena stands up. "Let's go. I have my water now."

"I'll carry those for you." Unhappily, I walk her home.

I don't see her for many days, choosing to spend my time with old friends. My mouth always feels sour and my stomach aches gently. My head is full of tiring, unhappy thoughts. Juman shows me the résumé he has written for me and says we are going next week to the City to look for jobs together. Kawsar says he can give me money for the trip. I am starting to think that really, I should go away, join a business or work in a factory, because there is nothing in the Town anymore, when I find out that Meena's husband finally divorced her properly and sold the house and everything inside except what belonged to her—her clothes and a comb.

಄

Meena sleeps on a blue-and-white sheet on a piece of ground by the river. On one side are her five jerrycans. On another is a small zipped-up bag and two or three plastic bags. She points to them and tells me what they carry: clothes, an extra pair of shoes, a mirror and comb, a towel, another sheet.

"You're free from him now," I say to her.

She glances at me but doesn't say anything.

There is a sense of freedom in me now when I go to see her. I can take her anywhere, give her anything.

I take her to see a movie. Meena and I walk side by side. I think about holding her hand. Instead, nervously, I talk about the sky and the yellow-brown buildings that look as if they are tilting, as if they've been arrested in motion. I tell her that the shops with the fluorescent tube lights are my favorite, cheerful squares of blue white. We pass by the barber giving someone a shave in the glare of an emergency light that he has suspended from a rope over the customer's chair. Close by, on the dirt, two men are sitting on plastic stools, a radio on one's lap.

The cinema is in the house of Khushi, an old classmate. It's one of his little businesses. He started this one when his father got sick. His mother used to sew wedding clothes for her clients in the City, but after Khushi's father died of diarrhea she stopped, saying that the *zari* and *zardozi* work gave her blinding pains in her eyes, as if she were being punished. She wanted to make simpler, plainer, humbler clothes now. But nobody bought those things. So Khushi partnered with a man in the City who was in the line of video cassettes. Copies of American movies and music videos. For a small fee, Khushi plays these in his room. Juman once tried to talk him into letting him be a part of this arrangement but Khushi smiled and shook his head.

When Meena and I arrive, she tactfully looks away while I pay my friend: three rupees for the first movie, and, for the second one, a bottle of painkillers Kawsar had found in a pile of trash near the hospital. Khushi is surprised who I've brought; his eyes become big in his face, which stays round no matter what the state of his belly. Meena and I go further into the house. There are long scarves and shirts draped over the backs of chairs and over the armrests. Khushi's mother rises from a chair, a needle and piece of cloth in her hands. She apologizes softly for the mess. "Are you here to buy? These are my older designs," she says. "The newer ones are at the back. Come see." We politely shuffle along behind her. The designs on the clothes get progressively chaotic. Geometric shapes and flowers at the front of the room, lopsided houses or circle-headed figures holding hands toward the back. Khushi's mother picks up a scarf with a wide stretched-out shape made out of black thread inside which are sewn small, uneven squares. "This is my smile scarf," she says. "I hope to take a suitcase full of these to the City when Khushi and I leave this town for good. I have heard they pay good money there for ethnic designs and patterns."

Khushi says, "These are beautiful, Ma." Gently, he guides her onto a chair. Then he ushers us into his room and shuts the door. He busies himself setting up the VCR and says, "Don't mind her. She keeps busy, it makes her happy." He turns off the bulb. The light from the TV fills the space in front of us. Later, on the way back, Meena says thank you, she enjoyed the stories even though she did not understand what they were saying a lot of the time. I close my fingers around hers and she does not pull away.

The next night I am sharing a smoke with some boys outside Chacha Ameer's shop when Khushi runs up to me and punches me in the face.

"What was in that bottle, kameenay? Baba Shah's wife says he threw up five times today."

My face hurts but I start to laugh at the thought of Baba Shah, dispenser of powders, getting sick.

Khushi snaps, "This isn't a joke. She wants his money back. You need to pay me."

"Come on, I don't have any, you know that."

He moans. "His wife said she'll poison my mother if I don't."

"She won't, she's just angry."

"Wait, I've got a little." Kawsar pulls a few coins out of his pocket and Khushi mumbles his thanks and shuffles off, stuffing them into his pocket. Chacha Ameer gives me the coldest thing he has in his store to put on my bruise, the bottom of his glass.

In the evenings I end up with Meena, sitting on the ground by her sheet. She reaches out and touches my face. The contact is too brief. I am left with only a ghost of her fingers on me. I cannot tell if her skin is cold or warm, smooth or rough.

"Have you started, you know, praying like one of them?" I ask, nodding toward a woman far away. It looks as if she is making ablutions in the water.

"I came here because I had little choice. But sometimes I think that maybe I am here because I really do need atonement." There is no pity or embarrassment in her voice, only matter-of-factness.

When I am with Meena, I watch her carefully for signs of illness or old memories, but she mostly likes to talk about the teachers I had in school.

"Some of them came from the City," I tell her.

"They must have been clever."

"We could live there one day. In a house. Together."

"You're going to marry an old woman?" She smiles.

"You're not old."

She doesn't say anything.

It is Chacha Ameer who tells me he has found a job for me. He says there is a man who sells tires a little way out of the Town who might be able to hire me. Chacha says I should give the man there his reference. He teaches me what I should say and lends me his good shirt. I hold it up in my room; a smell of talcum powder wafts up from the armpits. I get a ride in a rickshaw that is heading out; I tell the driver my father sends him his salaam. A lie, but it means the boy will not ask me for any fare. I find the shop Chacha had talked about. It is a small, dusty gift store. The man there listens to my practiced words, then tells me he's not looking to take on an employee, money is tight. But there is a tire shop at the beginning of the City that has recently expanded. I walk all the way to A.K. Tires, arriving there by noon, more irritated than thirsty. Mr. Asim asks me if I can start the next day.

ల౩

My boss likes to talk to me as we work. He seems to be a sympathetic man. He says my kind of life must be hard, and I tell him that my father is often away digging wells, and my mother is becoming weaker. I discover that I can make my voice sound young and burdened and brave. Mr. Asim, who rents a house in the City, says I am doing the right thing by shouldering the financial responsibility for my family. At the end of the week, when it's time for him to pay me, I don't remind him. I get on with tidying up the shop. When I am finished, I say, "Okay, boss. Salaam," and he says, "Wait. Don't forget your salary." Sometimes he adds a little extra in the roll of notes.

I don't spend any of my money, not even to buy cigarettes. Sometimes my boss gives me one. When my shoe splits a little, I cover the hole with electrical tape. My body becomes used to the long distance I go to work and back, and I do not tire out easily anymore. Mr. Asim brings his lunch from home, and he asks me to sit and eat with him. I am careful to take no more than a third, and of that I save some for my mother and some for Meena. I train myself to chew slowly.

Early on a Sunday morning Juman wakes me up. I have not seen him in a while; his eyes are red and there is stubble on his face. His clothes give off a smell of sleep. He is upset that Kawsar and I have no time to spend with him.

"How is your family?" I ask.

"My brother left. My other brother is convinced he's in the City but my mother thinks he's dead. My father has discovered that happiness lies in a bottle." Here, Juman gives me a grin, showing yellowing teeth.

When we get to Kawsar's house, Juman makes fun of his tight pants and his bright blue shirt. He says that as his wealthy friends we should be taking care of at least one of his meals. He lifts his shirt and shows us his ribs. I lie and say that I gave all my money to my mother and father. Kawsar slaps Juman on the back and says he will buy him lunch. I refuse his offer to do the same for me. There isn't any place in particular that we go to; we drift from shop to shop, exchanging nods and salaams with other Sunday drifters.

Toward the end of the day Juman asks, "Does your life have meaning now? Are you doing something important?" He is looking out over the road and his tone is gently mocking as usual.

"Might as well feed the belly a bit as long as we're alive, right?" Kawsar answers.

"Or you could not feed it and end it all much sooner."

"I don't know. I think we're meant to live as long as we can, no matter how we fill our days."

❧

My friends don't discuss Meena anymore, at least not in front of me. They ask me about my new job, but not what I do with the money. If they want to meet but I say I am busy they don't ask why or make jokes about women.

They bring her up only once. We are smoking cigarettes at the back of Chacha Ameer's shop; Kawsar holds his in his fingers and says, "If you ever need any help, you can tell us." Across from me, Juman dips his head low to indicate the same, the orange tip of his cigarette going down with him. I say to them, "I know." But I find it impossible to talk about her. I want to keep the details of our life—this new combination of hers and mine—to myself. What we say to each other and what we think about, I don't want to open any of that up to discussion and interpretation.

The weather changes on a Tuesday morning on my way to work, on that long stretch of road between the groups of shops. The cold wind enters my thin shirt so I run a little to warm up. The next time I wear two shirts but the wind is sharper. On Saturday night, on my way back from the river, I pass Chacha Ameer's shop. He is sitting on his chair, not eating, just staring at the slow-moving fan on the wall in front of him. I decide not to go in. A few meters away my feet kick a soft bundle. It is a sweater, large for me, but it smells all right and feels wonderfully warm. For a whole week I plan on giving it to my father but he is never at home, at least not while I am awake. I take it to Meena, along with the thin blanket from my bed. She accepts the blanket but refuses the sweater; she says it is a man's piece of clothing and she still has plenty of her own supplies.

She shows me her work. She has bored two sticks of wood into the ground diagonally, and tied her other bedsheet over their tops. "I weigh the sides down with stones at night and then I am warm inside," she says. I ask her again why she doesn't move into one of the rooms by the shrine, and she says that place gives her the shivers. "All those people pushing each other out of the way by the burial place, smelling of rosewater and sweat, moaning their prayers. It's different here; nobody is loud."

I leave the sweater with her anyway, and next weekend I go to a clothes market in the City. My boss told me about this weekly market where used goods are sold and I had said, "Good bargains for maids and sweepers, I'm sure." Along the four walls of a tent, the sellers have arranged clothes and shoes and bags and wallets on mats on the ground. I buy a warm shirt for my father and a shawl for Meena.

Back along the river I find a few more sticks and a cardboard box, which I open up like a boundary around Meena's area. Within this, she invites me to sit at the edge of her sheet, so I do, knees drawn up to my chest. I read her jokes from a week-old newspaper, and she splits peanut shells for us and laughs.

At the start of the new year I walk to the edge of the City in my found sweater and taped-up shoes and find Mr. Asim standing outside. Behind him, the grille cover of the door is still padlocked to the ground. He tells me he is closing the shop. "Because I got robbed last night, boy." He shakes his head, takes a deep breath. "They had a gun, took all my money." He waves his hands. "It was too close to the Town. You're a good boy, but it was too close to the Town."

5

VISITORS

On a morning in March, I go outside to find that the walls and telephone poles of our town have become covered with posters. Juman and I shuffle to a stop in front of a row of them, slowly and silently taking in the pictures and words. On each poster there are photographs of determined-looking faces of adults handing packages to a group of smiling children. Behind them is a picture of a pair of trucks with "Food" and "Clothes" printed on them. On top are the words, "Independence Day Outreach Program: City Delegation." I do not recognize any of the people in the photographs; they cannot be from this town. I run my finger over their faces; they are happy, and the paper makes them look glossy. I rip a poster off the wall and tear it again and again. At first Juman looks surprised, then he laughs and does the same. We run up and down along the wall, yelling and laughing and ripping up those faces and those words.

The day that the City visitors are supposed to arrive, on our national Independence Day, Kawsar stays in his house and Juman mumbles about needing to take care of something. But I want to see the new people, these saviors. They arrive in a calculatedly inconspicuous manner, in a bus at the main marketplace. They exit from that long white vehicle, putting out one foot onto the ground and then the other, warily looking left and right as if all the want and longing in the air here will overcome them. Some of them keep their eyes covered with sunglasses and I cannot tell what they are thinking. Followed by people holding microphones and cameras, they walk into shops, talk to the owners, shake their heads slowly when they hear things like, "My wife died when she was six months pregnant" or "My husband passed away from the sugar." Ragged children and a few adults hang around the visitors like flies. The entire group arrives at a sugarcane juice seller's cart, where his smeary machine is silent. "Closed," the man says, sitting on top of his cart, knees drawn up to his chin. "No more juice, no more money. My little children are starving." A City woman plunges her hand into her bag and withdraws a bundle of notes. She hands them to the man who presses his now-full hands to his chest, closing his eyes and murmuring his thanks.

This act by the woman seems to shift something in the visitors' group. They gather a little distance away by themselves and have a discussion with many gestures and shakes and nods of their heads. They are about to do something big. All of them start digging into their bags and wallets, and fistfuls of money emerge. *How is it that these people carry around this kind of cash?* I wonder, inching closer, not sure what they are going to do next. Will they toss the notes into the air and leave us to scramble to get as much as we can? One of them looks up, clasps his hands, and, in a loud voice, says, "Make a line, children, shaabaash, just as if you were in school, haha." Though I'm nearly eighteen, I step neatly behind a small boy. We haven't been told what to do next, but we understand instinctively what is expected of us—we hold out our hands. One by one, some money is put into each palm. The children run off laughing. When it's my turn, I say thank you in a low voice and walk off with dignity, not looking at the money.

What could I get with it? I could go to the edge of the Town and buy food, a kabab roll with a soda and chips, or a plate of biryani, even though I don't really like biryani, but a plate of it always looks like a lot; buy a pair of shoes like the ones the boys on TV wear; buy cologne, or a bicycle, or a car. I allow myself bigger and bigger things and my money grows with my wants. There is a program on TV where a husband and wife live in a big house. Water flows where one wouldn't have thought it could. In the front lawn there is a pond surrounded with flowery shrubs. A little way away stands a two-tiered fountain made of chalky white stone. Water splutters out from the top and cascades down like an unbroken, upside-down bowl. At the back of the house there is a swimming pool in the shape of a leaf. The inside of the house is even crazier. There are small curtains of water everywhere: between sheets of glass on the side of the staircase, on the floor in unexpected places, in bowls on tabletops. In the show, the owner is a rich woman. In my head, I make myself the rich person living in a house like that. That night in my room, I finally take out the money from my pocket. It is exactly one hundred and five rupees.

The visitors are most creative and industrious on the third day. In front of my old school they set up a small platform with a microphone. A man stands behind it, smiling benevolently at the people gathering below him. I am startled to see my mother among them.

"Thank you for welcoming us to your beautiful town," the speaker begins.

This is his first lie; our Town is ugly.

"In our very short time here we have learned so much about resilience and generosity," he continues. "We, including the wonderful Junaid sahab, have big plans to help you in your time of trial. Meanwhile, we the visitors would love to see the talents the people of this town have. I'm sure among you are reciters, jugglers, painters. Who wants to go first? Don't be shy!"

Somewhere in these words are his second and third lies. The more foolish among us grin and hesitantly approach the stage. A mother holds her little girl's hand and pulls her up the steps and says, "My daughter is very clever in painting sceneries. She will paint a scenery for you." From a large bag, a volunteer pulls out drawing paper and a set of watercolor cakes. She makes a great show of giving it to the daughter, while the man at the mic laughs and claps and urges the crowd to clap too. The little girl gets busy.

While she paints, a boy around my age walks onto the stage and says he can spit the farthest of anyone he knows. The mic man makes a face as if deeply impressed, though I am sure he must be cringing inside. He gestures to the boy to stand in a clearer space and says, "A talent is a talent. Ready? Start!" The boy puckers up his mouth and launches a ball of spit so small even the mic man cannot see it. The boy says he wants to try again, he wasn't able to get a good gob ready the first time. He shoots out another ball, but it is even smaller than the last one. The boy is upset. "I just need a bit of water to do a really good one. Can you get me a glass of water please?"

The mic man gently steers him back down the steps and into the crowd, saying, "Now don't worry, I am sure you are excellent at that, sometimes it is just not our day." By now the girl is done with her painting; the presenter holds it up for us to see. It is a collection of brown shapes standing on top of brown lines. "Very good, very good," the man says. I go home soon after. I don't know how long the spectacle lasts.

On their last day in the Town the visitors are to receive a grand thank you meal at the official building. The closer I get to it, the more people I see, also on their way. A *faqir* propels himself along on his wooden square seat with wheels underneath. We wave to each other. Our country's flag flutters on the roof of the building. It looks new. The grass on the lawn appears bright green. Flag-shaped buntings border the top edge of the walls. There is a large crowd there already. Those who got there early have their faces pressed against the gaps between the main gate and the walls. A few have climbed trees to see everything going on inside. I scramble up a trunk and sit on a branch. There are long tables set up on the perimeter of the lawn and four rows of chairs in the center. A small platform covered in white cloth or canvas has more chairs on it. The people walking around on the grass and among the tables look like staff; they are wearing a uniform of black pants and white shirts. A man with a close beard stands in front of the stage, consulting a piece of paper. He is wearing a stiff shalwar qameez and a waistcoat.

"Is that the one they call Junaid Ghani?" I ask a boy in the tree on my left. He nods.

The staff gets busier, quicker, moving in and out of the building through a side door. They bring out covered dishes and lay them on the tables. They emerge with trays of glasses, bottles of soda, thermoses, bowls, spoons, forks. Two men bring out pedestal fans and plug them into sockets. Then the main doors of the building swing open, and a large group of people walks out. I count thirteen of them. It is easy to see who the visitors are; they are all wearing blue shalwar qameez with badges on the front. Junaid Ghani rushes over to them, a smile on his face. He holds out his hands and bends a little at the waist as if to personally escort them all to their chairs. Once they are all seated, he goes up to the platform and gives a long welcome speech. He concludes by inviting someone to come up; he says a name but I do not catch it. Accompanied by polite clapping, one of the people in the blue clothes goes to the front and starts her own monologue. She says words about water, hunger, and compassion. She talks and talks and I gaze at them all. The City people don't look like the people from my Town. The faces of the visitors are plump and unlined, their voices rich. They sit with straight backs and steady smiles. How often do they wash? I wonder. Probably three times a day. And isn't their City by the sea? Not only do they have chicken and beef, they get fish, *the chicken of the sea*. It has been weeks since I have eaten meat. I am struck by how my people must appear to them. Our bodies are narrow and angular; our children's hair is uncombed. Boys wear pants with fraying cuffs, skinny ankles protruding above worn shoes. Men and women look chapped and wrinkled. Everyone looks dusty, everyone shuffles.

There is clapping again. The people in the lawn are now standing up and moving toward the tables; waiters are lifting covers off the dishes. The visitors are filling their plates with biscuits and pastries, picking up bottles of soda. Someone says, "Please take more food!" and they laugh and demur and refill. I smell the chicken and the sandwiches and the rolls. The murmurs around me on the other side of the wall rise in volume.

"I saw the van; all this came in the van. My uncle's cousin's nephew packed it himself in the big City," someone says. There is pushing at the gate. A girl on a branch below mine suddenly yells, "Thank you for coming to us!" Another voice shouts, "Give us some of that!" He means it as a joke, and most of us on this side understand that, and laugh.

Down on the lawn some of the visitors look up. One of them waves his pastry at us, a little unsurely. Perhaps he thinks we are crows and will descend upon him and his food. A woman begins to speak very rapidly to him; others around them lean in to listen. Now all the blue people are nodding and smiling. We in our trees shush those on the ground. "Listen! They are discussing something important!" we say. Below us, waiters are bringing plastic carrier bags to the visitors who start filling them with food from the tables. The watchers in the trees go wild with cheering; even those who can't see begin clapping as well. The visitors are now working faster, stretching bag after bag to capacity, their smiles widening into grins. When they begin to approach the gate my stomach spasms in hunger.

The Town people are now scraping shins and arms in their hurry to climb down the trees, joining those pressing against the closed gates. I try to push my way to the front as well. There is a cacophony of expectations around me; everyone is waiting for the gates to open and glorious food to be put into their hands; a man and a woman wonder what they will say if interviewed; a mother tells her son to talk to Junaid Ghani for a job, any job. And then a bag comes sailing over the wall, then another, and another. The mouths of the bags have not been tied; some of them cannot take the pressure of air and they open during their flight and for a moment we are still, watching the food come down. It hits the ground. Then there is a scramble as children and women and men try to grab as much as they can. We are crouched over feet and ground, collecting food, while being pelted with pastries and pieces of pound cake and samosas.

Someone misses a bag and it falls down. I reach out and grab it, screaming when a foot steps on my other hand. I press the bag against my chest, rise from my crouch, and push my way out of the crowd. I begin to run when I reach the edge of it, slowing down only as I near my street. Once there, I collapse onto the side of the road, my breath piercing my chest. Carefully, I part the bag's handles. Inside it are five small packs of chocolate sandwich biscuits. I tear open a packet and shake out two biscuits, cramming them into my mouth and chewing furiously. I am opening the third one when I become aware of a small, dust-covered child staring at me from across the street. I frown at him as I slowly eat my fifth biscuit. The child takes a step toward me and I jump up, stamp my foot and shout, "Shoo! Go!" I finish the rest of my loot more slowly.

It is only at night that I remember Meena. I try to ignore my guilt but the picture of poor, weak Meena who cannot even lift three canisters of water by herself, who sleeps outdoors with just a sheet between her and the sky, keeps coming back to me. I have to return to the grounds where the bags were thrown and hope there is something unclaimed still lying there.

My mother is slowly moving between the kitchen and the living room. She stops when she sees me walk toward the door. "Where are you going?" she asks.

"Out. To my friends."

"It is late." She crosses over to the door, not quite blocking it, her hand on the knob. I put my hand over hers, my stomach contracting at the touch of her papery skin.

"I need to go."

"Not tonight."

I enclose her hand in mine and lift it. There is no resistance, and that surprises me. I do not look back at her as I head away from the house. There is nobody out at this time of the night; there is no reason for anyone to be. I walk and run along unlit roads, a fresh hunger building up. When I reach the official building, I am surprised to find it in darkness as well. I go down on my hands and knees and crawl over the ground, feeling earth and torn paper from the buntings. Then the moon's filtered light makes something glint. I reach for it and find the comforting smoothness of packaged food.

I begin to walk away, clutching it in my fist, when the gravel shifts and a man appears out of the darkness. "That's for me," he says. He tries to take the package but misses and grabs my shirt instead. His face is inches away from mine; his breath is rancid, the ends of his long hair and beard uneven. He grins and says again, "That's for me."

I snarl, "Get lost," and kick his shin, and he laughs and loses his grip. But suddenly my hand is in his mouth, his teeth clamping down hard. Rage and pain make me scream, and I claw at his face. Again, he lets go and falls down. I grab his hair and slam his head into the ground. His eyes go blank, his arms boneless beside him. I stare at his chest but it is too dark to see if it is moving. I kick his side and there is no reaction.

I stumble away from his body, toward Meena by the river, my hand throbbing and the skin on my face aching, past dwellings that appear lifeless but out of which sounds escape into the night, startling me—a baby crying, a woman talking loudly. There is bile in my throat, there is the smell of the man on my face, his pathetic crumbling food is in my hands. I think about Meena and my legs turn to lead from fear of her leaving me. I think about her and my legs keep moving toward her, toward her place along the river.

There are no lights in the park. My footsteps sound loud over the dry ground; I try to run more softly. I get to Meena's cardboard home and tap on one of the panels. There is a sudden rustle from inside and a gasp. In a low voice I let her know it's me. Slowly, she lifts one end of the bedsheet-roof and peers out. In frightened whispers, like a child, I tell her about the man and show her the foil packet. She holds it up to the faint starlight.

"Milk biscuits," I whisper, reading the print.

She presses them to her chest. "Is he dead?"

"I don't know."

Quietly, her eyes on my face, she tears open the packet with her teeth. She pulls out a little rectangle biscuit and pushes it gently through my cold lips.

"I love you," she says. "Now go home."

❧

The visitors depart in their bus, and the Town looks browner and closer to death. We return to our dry-mouthed, concave-stomached sense of time. They had been here only for a few days but they had flooded us with so many treats that it felt like a month. Now, wherever I walk I see miserable faces and bodies: little children sitting dejectedly on the ground outside their shacks, disinterestedly chewing sticks or rolling rocks to each other; mothers with thin faces trying to feed their undergrown babies hidden beneath large pieces of cloth. Only my father carries on with the well work, even more energetically than before, leaving earlier and arriving God knows when.

The strongest effect of the visitors' leaving occurs when three children die in three different parts of our little Town. One of them is an eight-year-old boy who had been in the hospital for two weeks. Another is a fifteen-year-old girl from the jhuggi part of town, an asymmetrical collection of straw huts. She had gone to find some leaves for her little brothers and sisters when on the way back she fainted from hunger. Her body was discovered two days later. The person who found her said that with her ragged clothes and her narrow body she could be easily mistaken for a stick, which was the reason she wasn't spotted earlier. The third is a seven-year-old boy who got a stomach virus which made him vomit so much in the end he was heaving up air. He did this until his body gave up.

Junaid sahab goes to all three funerals in his brown Toyota. I see him at the last one, the one where the boy is put into the earth. Nobody stands near him; he looks too different from us. Afterward, at the boy's home where people come to pay their condolences, the wise elders sit on one side of the room, sharing a large sheet spread over the ground, while Junaid sahab is given a chair. Perhaps the worst thing about him, to me, is that his face is free of all expression. It is a careful face, which is a fact that does not work in his favor because he is a stranger here. Who has he lost? Who has he left behind? Does he hurt? Nobody knows.

Word goes around the Town that the deaths occurred because those spending time by the river are not doing it in the proper spirit.

Elderly people start worrying that people are doing wrong at a greater rate than the ones turning away from their bad ways. They hint that the City visitors have left more harm than good in their wake. Perhaps Junaid sahab should return to where he has come from, they mutter under their breaths. With the help of a few people they draft and put up a few posters over the old food truck ones. These carry one simple message: "The three best things to do every day are learn a new skill, practice an old skill, and keep away from dubious things."

In Chacha Ameer's shop one day I hear about the body of a man that was discovered by the milkman, who then gathered a few people to cart it away to the Town graveyard, where it was buried in the presence of strangers, nobody knowing who the dead man was and nobody having asked for him. The only thing about him which created a few hours' worth of news was his anonymity and the blood underneath his head. Nausea moves up from my stomach and I run outside. Only spit comes out, thickened with the remains of an old meal. When I tell Meena she says she has already heard this.

"Do you know where your friend Juman is these days?" she asks. There is an accusatory tone in her voice.

"The usual, I suppose. Maybe drinking with his father," I answer.

"I saw him in the park. He looked like he was headed toward the water. Had something under his arm, probably a mat. Probably means to spend time on it."

"Did he talk to you?"

"No. But you should give him a visit."

When I go to the park again, I don't look for Juman. Instead, I head straight to where Meena is washing her feet in the water. I put down the day's food that I've found for her and tell her that I want to marry her. She lifts her feet from the river and dries them on an edge of her thin towel, first the heel then the toes. Then she turns her face to me. Dark eyes underneath dark brows, giving away nothing.

"Okay," she says.

⁂

The next day, in front of my house, Meena waits by the motor-bike and watches me walk to the small gate and knock. It opens and my mother appears. Her eyes go from me to Meena, and before she even says anything she puts her whole body in the opening. She asks me what I want, why have I brought that whore to her house. I tell her I have just married Meena and we intend to live here.

"*My* house!" she shouts. "Not yours or your kameeni wife's." She spits at Meena, who does not move, does not make a sound.

My heart is beating in anger and fear. I try to say it is my father's house and I have a right to be in it, in my room, but all I can think of is when she had asked me to help her in the kitchen, and I had stayed. She keeps repeating "Get lost" in varying registers. I look at Meena; she hasn't moved, she stands as if transfixed. My mother steps back in and begins to push the gate shut. I start pushing back. But somehow I am weaker, or maybe I am the more defeated of the two of us. The door crashes shut. The squeak of the heavy bolt going across it is loud in the sudden vacuum made by our silences.

RAHEELA, 1966

1

THE GROCERY MAN

Suhail taught me how to get a bird to eat from my hand. The first time I tried this, the bird bit me on my finger and I gasped, but I was surprised to see my skin remain uncut. I tried many times after to see if I could make myself bleed, but though birds pecked at my wrist, my palm, my fingers, the blood never came.

The pigeons and parakeets lived on our roof in a series of interconnected cages. Suhail built them out of wood and wire along half a wall. He laid tiles on the top to keep the inside of the cages cool. Still another level above that was a wooden roof, standing on six tall rectangular poles. Inside, where the birds lived, he put small clay pots with parakeet-sized holes, bowls for water and birdseed, and bits of yarn and his own hair. He made a pretend tree out of twigs, binding the parts with twine and glue, and stuck it in the center.

Baba liked to help Suhail with maintaining the birds' homes. Baba worked at the meteorological office. I was very proud about this when I was young and told my friends in the street and at school. When I was older I learned that he was only an equipment technician there. He repaired instruments that went wrong. He came home from work around five every afternoon, took off his shoes and put on his slippers, untucked his shirt from his trousers, and went upstairs to the roof, calling out to Suhail as he climbed. If Suhail worried that it was hotter than usual, Baba brought up our pedestal fan for the birds. He plugged it into an extension cord which plugged into another one, which went into a socket at the base of the stairs. Baba and Suhail made sure the swivel switch was on.

Nabeela hated the large cage and the birds. She said they were dirty and noisy. Once, when Suhail was eight, she stormed up the stairs, stood next to Baba, balled her hands up into fists, and started imitating the coos of the pigeons and the shrieks of the parakeets, only much louder, and in an angry way. Suhail and I watched with our mouths open. Baba slowly turned toward Nabeela. She shouted, "I'm a bird! Look at me! Feed me!" Suhail giggled behind his hand, and I wanted to laugh too. Baba walked past Nabeela the shrieking bird and into the square mouth of the stairwell.

We were not rich, but our house was one of the more comfortable ones in the village. Suhail had his own room. It was small and he kept it tidy. One time Nabeela had tried to argue with our mother that it wasn't fair that the youngest should get his own room, but Mother told her it was because he was the only boy, and that shut up Nabeela. But Suhail preferred to sleep on the sofa in the living room anyway; he only used his little space on the days that he did not go to school and stayed in playing with his flimsy plastic toys. Nabeela, Aneela, and I slept in another room. A lot of times at night I crawled into Aneela's bed. She never told me to go away, and she never asked if I was scared or cold. Nabeela teased me about it sometimes in the morning. "Big, scared baby. Where's your milk bottle, little baby?" I retaliated only once; I kicked her leg, and, after she got over the shock and I got over my bravery, she twisted my arm behind my back until I cried. After that, whenever she teased me, I told myself that Suhail was my friend, not hers. He never went to Nabeela except when our mother or father sent him to her for something. If there was trouble at school, or if he was happy about a new book or a new toy, he came to me, and only me. I was too afraid to lose this exclusivity, so I never gloated about it to Nabeela, though it might have made her face flush.

One evening my brother took me outside and said in a very low voice that he had found a great source of food. "Where is it?" I asked him in a dramatic whisper, playing along. He took my hand and led me to the back of the house, where there was a tree which used to give us mangos up until two years ago. Suhail got down on his hands and knees at the base of the trunk and started to remove the earth with his hands. The soil was like a stale biscuit; the grains parted when he touched them. I sat down next to him and began to do as he was doing but he said, "No! You don't do this, Hil baji. That way Nabeela baji won't get angry at you when she finds out."

"But she'll get angry at you," I said.

"That won't matter in a few weeks. Nobody will be upset with me for long."

I did not understand, but I obeyed him and waited. A minute or so later, his small hands disappeared inside the earth. Suhail pulled up the handles of a cloth bag. With a surgeon's care, he untied them. "Look," he said. I leaned over and smelled the heady scent of chocolate before I saw it.

"What is all this, Suhail?"

"This is Nabeela baji's. I saw her here yesterday. Then she came back into the house, sweaty and dirty. I went out at night and dug around and found her things."

I was thrilled that we were taking apart Nabeela's secret together, that Suhail hadn't felt any pangs of love for big sister. "You did the hard work, you choose first," I said.

He took out a little cube covered with orange foil. "It's soft," he said.

I picked out a green, heart-shaped one. There were a few ants on both, but they didn't bother us. Neither of us had seen chocolate for months. We removed the foil, wiped off a couple of ants, and took a nibble. The warm, almost-melted chocolate spread over my tongue. I licked my lips and said, "I'm going to save the rest for later." I rearranged the green cover on my treat. Suhail shoved his into his mouth and put the wrapper in his pocket. I wanted to give him a hug, but he didn't like those at the moment. Instead, I said, "We should take one for Aneela" and took out a purple square. Suhail tied the handles of the bag and covered it up with soil. When we finally got up, it felt as if we had spent a whole afternoon crouching on the yellowed grass of our dying lawn, eating sweets.

If Nabeela found out about her ruined secret, she didn't mention it. For a few days, she walked about the house more quietly. Her look of worry made me happy. Suhail and I went on the dig a second time, at night, surprised and delighted to find the bag still there. After that Nabeela hid it somewhere else. And after that Suhail died.

I had only ever kept one secret from him. Our mother used to give me money to take to a shop that still sold imli. The shopkeeper was an old man, the uncle of a girl I used to play with once. He knew everybody in the town, including Suhail, but me especially well. That is because one day, when I was eight, I had come into his shop in tears; my mother had said to me earlier that I could not buy bubblegum, we didn't have the money. Mr. Anwar had given me a hug and rubbed my back, all the way from my shoulders, over my behind, down to the tops of my legs. Then he had given me a square of bubblegum and said I wasn't to pay for it and I wasn't to tell my mother or my father because they would only get angrier with me. And I wasn't to tell the other children because he didn't have enough sweets for all of them, only the ones he liked most.

"What about Suhail? And Aneela and Nabeela?" I asked him.

Mr. Anwar shook his head most emphatically. "They would especially get hurt! You don't want them to feel sad, do you?"

From then on, when I would go into his shop and it was empty, he would say to me, "Are you feeling all right today?" And right away I would be awash with sadness, and shake my head, and he would give me a hug and rub my back, always over my clothes, but sometimes squeezing lightly.

When he died a few months after Suhail, it wasn't because of a poetic reason like thirst, and it wasn't a graceful withering away of his body like that of the starving people. It was from a heart attack that he had while he was squatting over the toilet.

The day my brother fell into the well, Aneela didn't get out of her bed for a long time. I stayed next to her trembling body, and once or twice she reached out and held my hand. For a few days the rest of us—Nabeela, Aneela, and I—kept trudging up the stairs to the roof to feed Suhail's pigeons and parakeets. Our father had stopped taking care of them; we were worried our dead brother would be unhappy about this. But it seemed there were too many birds. They ate too much too fast. We were always feeding them. Then one afternoon I went up and found the whole cage empty; there wasn't a single creature inside. I ran back downstairs, my breath short and fast. Nabeela met me at the bottom, the big frown on her face making her look even older and sourer.

"Why are you calling out Suhail's name?" she hissed.

"What? I wasn't...the birds are gone."

She pushed me aside and ran up the steps and across the roof to the cage. "The door is open. They've flown away," she said, her voice a croak. "Somebody must have forgotten to close it."

"Suhail will be so angry, so hurt," I said, terrified that angels would tell my little brother the news in his grave and he would make his way out of it to harm us for not taking care of what he had believed needed a lot of love. I did not look at Nabeela. She didn't like it when I spoke about Suhail as if he were still living.

Then she said, "You're right," and marched to a corner of the roof and came back with a brick. She started hitting the wooden frame. Again and again she brought the brick down on it as hard as she could. I watched with my fists bunched at my sides, making small moaning sounds, until finally a square section broke and other parts began to give way. Now the wire was collapsing in places, onto the floor of the cage, over pigeon droppings and feathers and bits of seeds. Suddenly Nabeela turned toward me and I froze, terrified that she was going to hit me for just standing by. "Move away!" she shouted. I turned and ran down the stairs.

A little before Suhail passed away, the neighbors started whispering about us. They used to wonder how, in a village full of dying children, our parents still had all four of theirs, sleeping, waking, and moving around. None of us had contracted any of the diseases that other weak ones—the elderly and the young—seemed most susceptible to. We had become thin, yes; over our structures, our clothes hung loosely. And it was something that the clothes themselves were also not great; they had holes, or the thread was coming apart in the hem of someone's shirt, or the sleeve torn from the wrist to the elbow. But otherwise we stayed free of death.

I first learned about this kind of talk from Aneela, who came home one evening saying that a mother had stopped her on the street, knelt on the ground in front of her, and peered at her face and then at the palms of her hands. Then she had gotten up and parted the hair on Aneela's head. Eventually she had said, "Where does your water come from?"

"Except that she said *your* water," Aneela explained. "As if she thought we had a special well all of our own inside our house."

"What did you tell her?" Suhail asked.

"I told her it came from the same place as everyone else's, of course."

"The witch," Nabeela said. "The stupid witch. How dare she touch you."

Aneela shrugged. "She didn't hurt me. She was very gentle. And a little sad."

"Maybe we should send her some water," I said.

Suhail became indignant. "You know how hard it is for Baba to go down to the well three times a day? He eats the least of all of us and carries the most. She can get her own water."

On the day of his funeral, the lady who had examined Aneela came to our house to give her condolences. She patted my little sister's head and said, "Death comes to all of us, you see."

In bed at night, Aneela and I liked to make up details about the last day of Suhail's life: He woke up very early that day and did not change out of his most comfortable shalwar qameez because he did not care for fashion, or propriety. He left the house when the sky was still dark and hazy, as if touching it with a finger would shake loose morning colors. He walked almost seven kilometers to where the well stood, the pail empty and waiting. He leaned over to reach it but his body was too small. So, slowly, very slowly, he raised one leg and rested it on the rim, then tried to reach the pail again. But he lost his balance and fell down into the water.

I wasn't sure if Nabeela ever listened to us, but she always stayed quiet when we talked like that. Sometimes we added almost impossible descriptions. Aneela would make him a prince in a robe, or a man from space in a helmet. I would say the well was the passage to a secret palace, or the mouth to another planet.

Aneela's favorite story was that Suhail was traveling through a tunnel underground. He had a boat made out of wood which he rowed with a big plastic spoon that he found floating in the shallow river underneath the surface of the earth. Ammi didn't like it when Aneela talked like that. Sometimes she fed Aneela garlic to cure her, even though Aneela told me once that garlic made her head swim, garlic took her happiness away.

Sometimes Ammi said, "Aneela, my sweet daughter." Sometimes she cried. More often, she grabbed Aneela's braid in her hand and tugged it with just enough force to move her head back an inch or two, and hissed, "You are not allowed to speak like this in front of your father, do you understand?" My sister always nodded; she understood that Baba could not handle the fact that Suhail was all right but unreachable.

☙

No matter what kind of misery was going on, there was always a wedding to go to in the village. It was as if there was a race between how many lives were lost and how many new ones could be brought forth. Some people arranged marriages to *save* lives; they believed that the birth of a healthy child in a household was a sign of a good future for all under that roof. Everybody who could was producing babies. Newly married women, older married women. One time, a girl became pregnant but nobody knew the father. The girl's mother locked her up in her room, but some people came to visit her and convinced her to pardon her daughter and to see this as a blessing. So the girl was given a stern talk and allowed to come out of her room. Still, a lot of the new babies died, and a lot of new mothers died along with them, before them, or after them.

I went to a surprising wedding once, after Suhail died. The groom was a boy I had gone to school with. I recognized him from his name, and a little from the shape of his face and his eyes. He used to be the sad boy in my classroom, older than all of us. His father had died from a terrible and dramatic effort—he had set himself on fire or eaten poison, we weren't sure which. The boy cried every morning at his desk in the corner. I liked his curly hair and his unhappy brown eyes. I was moved by his tears. I used to sit next to him and offer him my sharpener and coloring pencils. I consoled him that his mother would return soon. The other children laughed at the two of us, said we wanted to marry each other. The English-and-math teacher ignored him but the science-and-Urdu lady tried to include him in our conversations.

"What makes you most happy? That is, what do you like best in your home?" she asked one morning. I was not yet ten.

The answers came. "My doll." "My father." "My cat."

"My toothpowder," the sad boy said, "and Raheela."

I was pleased, but that feeling lasted only a second before everyone burst out laughing. Was it the toothpowder? I did think it was an unusual choice of things to be happy about, but just a week before Manzoor had told us in a whisper that he had eaten a third of the powder from his bathroom shelf.

Confused, I looked at the teacher. She was smiling. Gently, she said to the sad boy, "Raheela does not live in your house."

He gave me a terrified look; he had embarrassed me in front of the whole class and now I wouldn't be his friend anymore. But I understood my liking of him and his extreme need of me far more than I understood the reason for my classmates' laughter. I smiled at him and gave him a small wave.

Sitting now on the special chair next to his bride, dressed in his fancy, passed-down clothes, he still seemed a little lost to me, a little worried. It was in the way he was blinking, I realized. Two fast blinks, then pause, then two quick ones again. Suddenly he was looking at me. I wanted to tell him about Suhail. I smiled and waved but he turned his head away. Perhaps he didn't remember me.

2

A FUGITIVE STREAM

MY SISTERS LIVED ALONGSIDE ME, each in her own sphere. Often, we didn't know what to say to each other. One day, though, we became friends, briefly. A woman came to visit our mother. Through the drawing room door, we heard the two speak about the state of the village, a new township being started by some near the City, her husband's small plot of land there.

Then the woman said, in a tone of sisterly confidence, "I would like to have Aneela for my son."

Between us, Aneela's body stiffened, and Nabeela and I squeezed her shoulders.

Our mother said, "Not Nabeela? She is twenty years old. She is very clever and knows how to run a house with thrift."

"No, sister. It is Aneela I want."

"Not Raheela? She is sixteen, just the right age for starting a new life."

"No. My son says he heard her talking to herself one day."

Ammi sighed. "Aneela is too young, only thirteen. Just a child."

"And my son is twenty. Just the right age difference." The woman's voice became sweeter. "Think about it, sister. Plenty of babies, plenty of improved fortunes for both the families. I heard your husband lost his job in the City."

"We are quite all right here." We heard the creak of the sofa; Ammi must have gotten up. "Let me get you some water before you go. Unless you prefer soda, or tea. We have all three."

My sisters and I fled to our room and fell onto one bed—Nabeela's—and she did not tell us to get off it. I looked at her; her face was full of laughter. She made her voice deep and said, "I want you for my warty son."

I clasped my hands and knelt before her. "Please, ugly mother of ugly son, I am too young."

"I don't care. We're all out of blessings. We've been very bad. You're our only cure." Nabeela pretended to gobble up my hands. Aneela doubled over with laughter. But later that night, when I couldn't sleep, I climbed into Aneela's bed and saw the whites of her eyes in the dark.

"Ammi was lying about the soda and the tea, wasn't she?" she asked, her voice a whisper.

"Of course."

"And the water."

"Yes."

"I think, Raheela, we are out of blessings."

I giggled, thinking that she was being funny like before. But I stopped when Aneela didn't laugh. "Nabeela was just joking about that, you know that," I said.

"I think we've been very bad. That's why we're running out of things and people. Someone has to do a bit of sacrificing."

"You're not thinking of marrying that idiot, are you?"

"No, not that."

Aneela closed her eyes then, and after lying next to her for a few minutes, feeling irritated at her seriousness after our rare lighthearted moment earlier, I quietly went back to my bed. In the morning, Ammi didn't mention the woman with the proposal. Baba went off to

Chacha's farm, and my sisters and I cleaned up the house a little and helped Ammi make some food for later. Around six in the evening, Aneela said she was going to say hello to her friend who was just outside the gate. She walked out of the front door and did not come back.

Baba went to the City to look for her and took me with him. We walked around for hours, checking faces of passersby and of people on billboards; she could be anyone or anywhere. Before we got on a bus to come back to the village, Baba left a photo of Aneela with the police.

My mother was a woman of iron. Years ago, after she had given birth to Suhail through surgery and was supposed to rest for a month, she was back on her feet in a week, feeding him and cleaning the house and carrying home the grocery. In their inability to be broken she and Nabeela were alike. The two of them moved through their tasks with efficiency and brusqueness. I spent my days in bed, getting up only occasionally to go to the bathroom or the kitchen where I ineffectually moved pots and pans around. Once I set some water on boil and went back to my room. I woke up to the sounds of shouts; the pot had begun to burn and smoke had filled the house.

Baba moved us to the City. He went there first to start his job as a driver in a big company. We waited to hear from him that he had found a home and we should come. In those weeks, time blended for me; mornings into afternoons, nights back to mornings. Sometimes I walked around the village. I wasn't looking for anything or anyone, food or brother or sister. I passed by the rooms that used to be my school, by the house of a girl who used to be my friend, by the shops I used to get my mother's things from.

Baba came to get me, Nabeela, and our mother at the bus depot in the City. I tried not to stare at the people rushing and pushing around; I didn't want to look like an ignorant girl from the village. I put on what I thought was an expression of indifference. But Baba was excited and kept asking me and my sister what we thought about it all, wasn't it exciting, so I had to readjust my face to show my true feelings every time he turned toward me. We took a rickshaw to our house. The only way all four of us fit in the backseat was because we were mostly bones, especially me. Our suitcase was partly over my lap and partly over Nabeela's. Baba grinned and said that would keep us from falling out. He and my mother carried a large gathri each on their laps. The rickshaw driver was fast. Nabeela dug her fingers into the top of the suitcase but I only lightly rested mine on it, wishing I were sitting on the door side, my face inches from the road rushing away beneath me. I inhaled the exhaust fumes; the smell was thick and old. I wanted the fumes to envelop me.

On and on we went, along wires strung between poles, sometimes drooping all the way to the road, sometimes unattached from the next one, having given up on holding on to it; along posters and black lettering on walls. Sometimes our rickshaw was in the middle of the road, and there the fumes were the strongest. Nabeela covered her nose and mouth and pressed herself into the corner but I turned my face into them and breathed in deeply. After almost an hour I woke up. We were next to railway tracks. There were children here, barefoot and curious about us. There were no other cars, only a line of single metal doors on the left, some cracked open. I glanced through as many as I could, catching glimpses of rooms. Baba told the driver to stop in front of one of them. Nabeela pushed the suitcase off our laps and sideways, letting it fall out through the doorway. Slowly, she climbed out, muttering under her breath like an old woman, fixing her dupatta. Baba unlocked the plain black door, and we stepped into our new dark rooms.

My mother, Nabeela, and I slept in the bedroom. Baba insisted upon sleeping in the living room. This was because there was a two-burner stove there underneath which stood a gas cylinder. He said it was dangerous for us to be there. Nabeela complained at different times throughout the day. She was upset about the size of the house, about not knowing anyone here, about being stuck with a sour little sister. It was not hard for me to ignore her. Mostly I thought about Aneela. I imagined she had made her way to this City and once again she and I were within the same perimeter. When I was feeling happier, usually after a meal which involved rice, I was able to make Aneela's hair shiny and her body fuller, in my mind. When I was grumpy or too warm, I was unable to dig her out of the earth. Only once, after I was sure our mother was asleep, did I mention her to Nabeela. I asked, "Do you think maybe she is married?" Nabeela raised herself on an elbow, hit my face, then turned her back to me and went to sleep.

Baba put me in a government school. The first few times, he did the whole journey with me, catching the minivan to the bus stop, then getting off near the school, then getting on a rickshaw which took me to the school gates. Baba said his boss didn't mind him showing up an hour later than he was supposed to. "He is such a good man," he said. But one night he told us that he had received a warning at work about his lateness. That's when Ammi started taking me to school. With a finger in my big sister's face, she told her, through gritted teeth, to keep the door locked and not even think about stepping out, not even if our house was on fire. With Ammi, all the parts of the morning before I entered my school began to feel interminably long. She never smiled, never talked unless it was to say whip-like sentences: "Keep your eyes on the road" or "Pick up your pace."

The families that the girls in my school belonged to were different from the ones in my neighborhood. There, the mothers usually worked as maasi in the homes of people in the City. Ammi said our father had a very respectable job as a driver and we had our own house back in the village and she was never going to wash anyone's toilets. I was glad to hear her say it. I considered myself more like the girls in my school, even when a group of them asked me where I lived and then, when I told them, never spoke to me again. But I didn't blame them; they just didn't know about my house back in the village, one of the nicest ones there. At a school function where we didn't have to wear our uniform, I saw their clothes. They had not been handed down to them through their mothers by their employers; they had been stitched by tailors or their mothers, using lace and fabric bought in shops. Mine, too, had been made by my mother or my aunts. Even when I wore what used to belong to Nabeela, it was something that had once been made for her. So we were not so far apart.

There was a girl in my class I liked a lot. Her name was Runa. Her nails were long, slim ovals on which she wore clear nail polish so the teachers couldn't catch her. She always had on tiny earrings, and her eyebrows were neat, thick arches. I lent her a pencil once. The next day, during recess, she took me aside and picked up an end of my braid.

"I like the color of your hair," she said. "Brown." She dropped my braid. "Where are you from?"

I told her.

She said, "I liked your qameez at the function. Too long and loose, though, for the City. Ankle-length shirts have not been in fashion for a very long time now. Two years, at least. Bring your qameez to school tomorrow."

In the bathrooms the next day, I held the daaman of my shirt taut between my hands while Runa cut off most of it from the hem up. "Try it on," she said. Inside a stall, I swapped my uniform for my altered shirt. Outside, seeing my reflection in the mirror, I gasped. The new hem was just skimming my knees. At home, I altered two more shirts, staying up late after everyone had fallen asleep, working in a sliver of streetlight behind the curtain. Runa taught me excuses that the teachers would believe.

"Tell Mrs. Fauzia you've started your period and need to go to the bathroom."

"But I haven't got my period yet."

"You mean today or ever?"

"Ever."

"You're lying."

I shrugged. "Lots of girls from the village don't get their period till late."

"I got mine at twelve. Most girls here do."

I crossed my arms.

Runa said, "It doesn't matter. Just make it up. It's not like they're going to check."

Still, there were teachers who believed us or did not care, and teachers who would have contacted our parents. Every other week, before the last hour of school, Runa and I went to Mrs. Fauzia and complained of headache or stomachache or dizziness or period, and she nodded absently and waved us off. In the bathroom, we changed out of our uniform, put on pink lipstick, covered ourselves with chaadar. We sneaked out of the school from the kindergarten side and walked to a shop on the corner. There, our friends Jamaal and Hamid picked us up.

They were older than us and went to another school. Runa said she had met them at a tuition center last year. It felt strange the first time I climbed into a boy's car. Runa sat in the front with Jamaal. In the back by myself, I placed my palms on the smooth cover of the seat. The inside of the car felt and smelled cold.

"Are you new here?" Jamaal asked.

"Yes," I said.

"What do you think about it all?" He made a careless gesture, a half-wave of his fingers, toward the windshield.

"The trains are loud."

"He means the City," Runa said.

"I haven't really seen all of it," I said quickly.

Jamaal drove and Runa chatted with him. Once, when his hand was on the gear, her hand strayed over and covered his. It was a brief moment after which she moved it to turn on the radio. A while later, Jamaal stopped by a large, square house and blew the horn. I fixed my hair and rearranged my dupatta; I wanted to borrow Runa's mirror but didn't want to call attention to myself.

The boy who came out of the gate was tall and thin with very curly hair. He slid into the backseat with a grin, slapping Jamaal on the shoulder. He said hello to Runa in a familiar way, an old acquaintance way. Then he turned to me, and I found I could talk and laugh the way Runa did. That became our seating arrangement: Runa and Jamaal in the front, Hamid and me in the back. Sometimes the boys bought us French fries, sometimes a whole lunch, and felt our hands: a thumb over the back, across the knuckles, and down each finger, then drawing circles on the palm. The first few times all four of us met, that was what we did. Then one morning at school Runa gave me a shaving stick and taught me how to remove the hair from my arms and my legs. She showed me how to pluck hair off my upper lip with a thread. "Don't touch your eyebrows, your mother will find out," she warned. I became a whole new secret body.

The next time Jamaal picked us up, he took us to Hamid's house and said we were going to spend time inside, maybe watch a little television, maybe talk about ourselves. Hamid showed me all the rooms. They were big, but I had seen bigger ones in the village. I could tell rich, and Hamid's family wasn't it. I wanted to tell him about my chacha's farm. Until some years ago he had grown wheat and cotton and kept buffalo for milk for the family. The low brick wall around his farm and house was never painted but it went around a larger area than the wall of this City boy's house. My chacha had to pay eighteen lacs to the seller before the land, the crops, and the animals could be fully his.

When Hamid showed me a black-tiled bathroom, I pretended to be impressed. I liked the living room though. The sofas were deep, the carpet soft even if a little worn out. Hamid pulled the curtains across the windows and turned on the big television. A woman with her hair in a braid was running down the stairs, calling out, "Baba! Baba!" I could not get absorbed in the story because Hamid was sitting next to me. And just a few minutes later Runa and Jamaal got up and left. Now I couldn't hear the drama on the screen at all over the noise of my nervous thoughts. I was annoyed at Runa for her thoughtlessness and I was sweating through the cotton of my good green qameez. But Hamid did nothing at all, just kept sitting on his side of the sofa, and the scenes rolled on, one after the other. And when the other two returned for Jamaal to take me and Runa back to the tracks, I was both relieved and disappointed.

I got used to it all: the pretending to my mother, the pink lipstick (the only color Runa seemed to have), the sofas in Hamid's house, the flow of water when I turned the tap, any tap, watching dramas on Hamid's TV, going with him into his room, coming out and eating a piece of fruit from his kitchen. There was always something to eat.

Hamid liked to close his hand around my arm and make his thumb touch his finger. He said I was so thin if I stood behind his bedroom door he could swing it open all the way toward the wall and I would still have space. We tested this, and it was true. He sometimes said, "You don't completely look like a girl from the village. You don't look like you're from here either. You're more of an in-between girl." Sometimes he asked me to describe to him the meals I used to eat in the village.

"I've told you so many times already," I would say.

"Tell me again."

"Do you want the good times meals or the bad times meals?"

"Bad times, please." And he would lean back on the sofa, rest his head on his arms, close his eyes, and listen.

Then, one day when we met, he told me he hadn't eaten anything for two days. The last meal he'd had was a very early, very simple breakfast.

"Come on, you must have had a Cola or something," I said.

He shook his head and grinned. "Not a single thing."

And he asked me to cover up my face, and he did the same, and we went on a long, hot walk. When we came back, sweating and thirsty, he croaked out, "See, I can live the way you all do." He started watching TV but soon he was holding his head in his hands, his head gripped in a band of pain. "It hurts everywhere," he whispered, his eyes squeezed shut tight. I got him a bowl of rice from the refrigerator and he stuffed handfuls of it into his mouth. After that day, we went back to the regular things we used to do.

Hamid liked to show me around the City. The sea, the roundabout with the four fountains, the port area.

"Where is Kam Paani?" I asked him once.

"That's just a little stream, not a pretty place. An ephemeral stream, in geographical terms. A fugitive stream. Only runs when it's rained a lot."

"What does it run into?"

"The sea, of course."

I liked how Hamid and I were different from Runa and Jamaal. Still, when Runa told me that Jamaal liked to buy her things, I was a little jealous.

"What kind of things?" I asked.

"Perfume, bangles." She shrugged. "Last year he insisted on buying me new shoes for Eid." She stuck out her feet and giggled. "Aren't they pretty?"

I looked at her black sandals with the short heels, now several months old. Curiosity overcame my jealousy.

"What did you tell your mother?"

"She never asked. They're not that different in shape from my other black shoes, I suppose."

The next time I was with Hamid, on his sofa, I thought, *My arms are so bare. My shoes are so old.* I felt very sorry for myself. I tried to eat the words that rose upon my tongue, and focus instead on the dirty-faced man on the screen speaking urgently to a dirty-faced woman, but then an explosion went off and cars flew into the air and the woman's body flew in an arc and her shoes went with her, and I said, loudly and tearfully, "Why don't you ever buy me gifts?"

The first thing he bought me was a bottle of perfume. An emerald-green rectangle glass bottle with the words Dark Love on it. I pulled up the stopper and sprayed a little onto my wrist. It smelled strong, stronger than I liked. There was an unmistakable artificiality about it; no woods or flowers could smell like this unless they were rotting. But I replaced the stopper, shoved the bottle into my handbag, and smiled at Hamid. Pleased by my reception, he said, "The building where this shop is was built in 1796, can you believe it?" I kept the perfume for five days before throwing it into the trash heap close to my house.

He got me a hair clip, a magazine called *Stories for Women* (which I threw away), a pair of metal earrings with fake black stones set in them (from a man who sold jewelry to starlets, Hamid said), a plastic bracelet (which I threw away), a small diary (which I slipped inside another girl's bag in the school). I used a safety pin to attach the earrings to the inside of my shirt. When I sat with my mother, father, and Nabeela in the evening, I pressed the metal into my body. The cool, sharp sensation took me away from the droop of my parents' backs, the anger on Nabeela's face, and the ghosts of Aneela and Suhail who quietly joined us.

The rain, when it came, was different from the one I had seen in the village years ago. In the City, the sky became a more tempestuous gray. It rained hard for two days. By the time it stopped, so much water had collected on the roads that the traffic had to stop and people had to leave their small cars and gather on the side, where they shook their heads and laughed. Ammi and I, on our way back from school, had to get out of the rickshaw and wade through the water to get to where we knew the footpath was. Drenched from the waist down, holding our bags to our chests, we got into a bus that was bravely and slowly sloshing from stranded person to stranded person.

I asked Hamid if we could go to the stream, just the two of us. In the car, he grinned and squeezed my hand frequently. The street the stream was on was a very quiet one, thick with trees. Hamid stopped the car under one of them. He started to turn toward me but I opened the door and jumped out. I was at the low wall, taking off my shoes, when he jogged over.

"What the hell are you doing?"

"We can go swimming there." I pointed at the water. I ran along the wall until I found a place where the bricks had broken off. I climbed over, landing on damp earth covered with flattened plastic bags and rags and leaves. The water smelled musty but it was mostly clear. I walked into it slowly; its warmth surprised me.

"I'm going to wait here until you're done being crazy," Hamid said. He stood on the edge, his arms hanging down by his sides. "Do you even know how to swim?"

I laughed. "I don't know."

Hamid began taking off his jeans and his shirt. Then he waded in. "Now I don't know what the hell *I'm* doing. Crazy witch."

Slowly, I moved my body until I was on my back, floating. I felt my hair stream out behind me. Maybe Aneela had gone this way, looking for Suhail. She must have kept her body close to the walls in the village, made herself undiscoverable. She had always been as narrow as the drains, the narrowest of us all. She might have come here and seen that discarded banana peel and that water-stiffened magazine on the bank, and imagined that Suhail might have eaten and read here a while before swimming on.

Runa said to me one day at school that she was in love with Jamaal and would not mind if she were to die just then because she felt so complete.

"I would like to marry him, we would have such a good life," she said. "I'll have to make sure his mother likes me, doesn't mind where my family lives."

"Isn't she a professor somewhere? Of Urdu literature? She's probably broadminded."

"Do you think you love Hamid?" Runa asked after a pause.

"No, I don't think so."

"What, even after all this time?"

"I mean I *could* love him."

"Yes! He takes care of you, and his house is so nice."

"It's all right. But I wouldn't *mind* loving him."

Six months later, Baba was let go from his job. He didn't want us to have to go back. He said he was worried I would never finish school if we did. But I knew the other reason he wanted to stay. He did not want to be far from Aneela; he believed she was here somewhere in the City, in an alley or a room or the garden of a big house, as an unsheltered girl or a working one. Even if he thought she was a buried girl, he wanted to be near her.

While he looked for means for us to stay, I cried. I cried to Runa, and she also wiped her eyes and said she would never forget me. I cried to Hamid, and he pulled me onto his lap and promised he would come to the village and find me and take me away with him. I didn't believe him but, at that moment, if Runa had asked me again if I loved him, I might have said yes.

A few days later, Baba told us he had found work but the money wasn't enough to keep me, my sister, and our mother in the City as well. The three of us would live in the house in the village while he stayed behind. I begged my father to let me stay with him. I wailed that I would die if they made me go back. I wiped my nose on my sleeve and promised I would not mind living in a one-room house and eating one meal a day, a week. Nabeela put her hands over her ears and went into the other room. My mother slapped my face and twisted my ear and, through gritted teeth, warned me to keep my voice low.

Runa was sympathetic, but by the end of that last week she was perhaps bored with the specifics of my life and started spending more time with other girls. I asked her to help me meet Hamid, and she said she would. But only Jamaal came by. He said Hamid wasn't well but he had sent me a message. I grabbed the folded piece of paper from him and opened it. GOOD LUCK, I WILL MISS YOU was all it said.

My mother, Nabeela, and I left on a Saturday morning, sitting in the bus in silence. We were a family that had achieved mixed results in trying to improve itself; three-quarters of us had come back to rejoin our dying village. The money my father sent was useful. For a while, I went to school in the village, the same one-room operation I had left. Only now there were even fewer children attending it. I didn't care. Whenever I could, I imagined I was in the City, with Hamid, Runa, and Jamaal. I held brief conversations with them in secret murmurs. "That film wasn't very good" or "Should we pick up some rolls from that new restaurant?" In my mind, my hair was loose because I had gone to a beauty parlor with Runa during our lunch break. There was no ugly growl in my stomach from lack of food, and I walked, not shuffled.

About a year after this, my father came back and my sister and Noor, a daughter of one of our uncles, left for the City. Nabeela had gotten a chance to work there as a teller in a bank, and our cousin Noor was to become a teacher in a primary school. Later, Noor left her job and started modeling for a beauty products company. Meanwhile, I turned seventeen, and a good woman in the village sent my mother a marriage proposal on behalf of her nephew, who was a good man. His name was Masood. When I got married to him, my cousin Noor sent me six tubs of blemish-removal creams as a present.

RAHEELA, 1996

1

THE DOCUMENTARY

I HAVE STARTED GOING OUT AT NIGHT sometimes to see what I can find to eat. I cover up well with a chaadar over my face; I don't want anyone recognizing me. I go to little, closed-up general stores, to homes with people still living in them. I have been reasonably lucky so far. I have found a bag with a few tablespoons of stale cooked rice in it, probably meant for birds, half a hard naan, a few beans. I am very good about sharing with Masood whatever I find, even though he doesn't bring home much in return, not anymore, not since Baadal went away.

I had a worry the other day; I realized I hadn't had my period at all for two months. I knew it could not be because of a baby. Later, while I was looking through a garbage bag behind the official building, I remembered that when I was young, I didn't get my period until I was well past fifteen, and that was not unusual. Our mothers had fed us mixtures of powdered roots with prayer words whispered over them, afraid that we would grow into incomplete women. But most of us did get our cycles, and though we were relieved we were also disappointed at what we had to manage: the pain, and changing a bloodied rag for a clean one, and keeping the growing pile of them far from the noses of any men in the household so they wouldn't retch from the smell. As I walked back with a packet of biscuits that had turned mostly into crumbs, I decided this current lack of bleeding was an ease, a cause for celebration.

At home, I waved the biscuits in front of Masood's face. "Look what I found." He waited for me to move away from the TV screen. I shrugged and made sure the wrapper made a loud crinkling noise as I opened it. I picked out the larger pieces and put them in my mouth and said, "Mmm. Delicious." But he kept on watching the weather report. I licked the rest of the packet clean. He never even turned his head. I got an image in my head of my son sitting with ease in another house, face turned toward another TV. Just like his father. I was as a ghost to both of them. My feeling of triumph vanished, and I felt hungry and hollow again.

The charity liaison officer's cleaning woman has left. I found that out when I went to one of the marketplaces hoping to exchange my nose pin for bread. It is a simple thing, my nose pin; there is no jewel in it. But I cleaned it well and put it in a little box and took it with me to Chacha Ameer's shop. I went to him because I have heard he is a kind man. He did not disappoint; I came away with some flour in a pouch and a few tablespoons of sugar. He also told me about the vacancy in the official building. I nodded as if I did not understand that news was meant for me, as if I were meant to pass it on to a truly needy person. But something terrible happened later that afternoon. I wasted all of the new sugar and flour. I should have been more careful and prudent, but I got the taste for sugar bread in my mouth and so I made small circles out of my precious new ingredients and poured the dark brown oil in the pan and turned on the fire. The moment I put my circles in, they became limp and heavy-looking instead of light and airy. When I took them out, I saw they had little black spots on them. Still, I tried one. It tasted very bad; my tongue got coated in oil. I sat on the floor and took another bite and cried and took another bite and cried some more.

I saw the charity officer out in the Town today. He was with another man. They were slowly walking in front of the line of shops in the main marketplace, hands behind their backs except when one of them stuck out an arm to gesture toward a shop or an electricity pole or us, the watchers, our movements arrested by the presence of these men. The officer's face is serious but not unpleasant. His clothes seemed expensive to me, a better variety of cotton than I have seen anyone in the Town wear. He is not tall, and he has a close beard. When he turns his head to glance over the small clump of people that I am part of, I cannot help myself—I hold my breath and wonder if he will notice my face. Man from the City. Government man. That night, I imagine the scene in the marketplace: he notices my face, and his arm pauses midmovement.

My interview with the charity officer is simple. Can I put away files and do light dusting and cleaning? I say yes. Can I start right away? Again, I say yes. "How much salary do you normally take?" he asks me, and I tell him I am not going to be working as his cleaner or maid but as an assistant, and if he likes he can assist me back with some food. He looks puzzled, and opens his mouth, then closes it. "As you wish," he says. He shows me where the bucket and mop are kept, and then goes inside his office and softly shuts the door. It is a matter of an hour cleaning the bedroom and the living room, the only two rooms that are open. I would have finished sooner but I do not want to go home. So I dust each book, and stand on a chair and clean the tops of the cupboards, and I run the cloth over the leaves of the fake plants. The whole time, Junaid stays behind that shut door. Not once does he call out for me. He never even coughs. Once, I hear his phone ring, and I stop moving. His voice comes through the door as a soft mumble, then with a click the receiver is set down and he is quiet again. When I am done, I knock to let him know I am going. For a few seconds there is no sound, then a chair's legs scrape over the floor and the door is opened.

"Thank you," Junaid says and hands me a cardboard box.

"What is this?" I ask.

"Almonds. This is all I have at the moment."

"You don't want to check the work?"

"No, no, it's fine, I'm sure. Same time tomorrow?"

"Yes."

⁓

Every day I get to Junaid's office-residence by eleven, walking as fast as I can. There is an abundance of good things in that place—the sofa cushions are firm, the lighting is bright and unflickering, and all the corners it shines on are clean, not crusted over with sad-looking dirt. The cleaning supplies are from the City; I haven't seen these bottles of floor cleaner and toilet cleaner in the Town. The room where Junaid sleeps is very simple. There is a single bed, a small table, a mirror with a glass shelf under it, and a one-door steel cupboard. I cannot tell if he is a religious man; there is no prayer rug or book of scripture that I can see. Maybe he keeps them locked up. I love the bedsheet on his bed; it is midnight blue, and so tightly woven I cannot see the mattress even when I put my face close to the threads. I am allowed to fill the bucket a third of the way with water, which is far more than I get from my tap at home, and far more than any amount of dirty water Masood has ever brought back in a bottle from one of his poison-filled wells. I like how the whole place smells once I'm done cleaning it. That is another plenitude. I always start with the bathroom. I shut the door and move the little latch across to lock it, slowly and softly. I turn on the tap, careful not to apply too much force to it, letting the trickle become a thin stream. I adjust the flow until the water coming out slides down the wall of the sink and into the drain, making no sound at all. I wet my hands, then bring them up quickly under my shirt and move them over my chest and my stomach. I wet them again and reach around and rub my back but my muscle feels uncomfortable and I am afraid to sprain it. Lastly, I wipe my armpits with my dampened hands. I turn off the tap and unlock the door, then with a lot of noise I tilt the bucket and let the water flow over the floor.

When I am cleaning the bedroom, he stays in the office. When I clean the office, he goes to the bedroom. He is very proper and respectful. He has not spoken a lot to me, and the food he gives me at first is unimaginative. A bar of chocolate, or a paper bag of samosas gone slightly stale. But lately he has been bringing me proper meals. Mutton or chicken curry with rice, or daal and achaar. I accept it with thanks, but not too much of it because I am not his servant. Afterward, I go to the end of his street, use a spoon to move a little bit into a bag for home, and leave the rest in front of Meena's house. That is where I believe she and Baadal are. I have never rung the bell.

Masood sighs noisily whenever I put out food from the officer's house.

"Go on, sit with me. Eat. You're looking more like a skeleton every day." A wave of the old affection comes over me. Such a poor-looking, thin man.

"So terrible that you think you have to work for food," he says in a sad voice. He starts putting on his shoes.

"I do it for us, for Baadal." My voice cracks. "You feel free to carry on with your selfishness, meanwhile."

"Baadal and his wife are in Juman's house."

I see me creeping up to Meena's house with food for my son who hasn't even been there. Embarrassment chokes me. "How do you know?"

"He came to see me. He said they were moving to the City. He looked happy."

He is saying something else but I stick my fingers into my ears and yell, as loudly as I can, "I cannot hear you! I cannot hear you! Go away! Go away!" over the shuffles of him getting ready to leave, over his goodbye.

One morning, soon after that, I wake up and my first thought is: it has been a few days since I have seen Masood. My second thought is: I would like Junaid to speak to me. I survey the few clothes on hangers in my cupboard. The prints have become faded and the material thin with repeated washings. I wear what I think looks the least old: a green shalwar qameez suit. I comb my hair and, when I twist it into a bun, I do not do it in the usual haphazard way; I take care to settle it onto the nape of my neck. Maybe in a moment of carelessness I will leave my head uncovered and he will happen to see me as I have not been seen in years. I am excited and nervous as I go to the official building. A very long time ago, when I was a girl going to school, I used to sometimes feel like that. But nothing of significance happens at Junaid's office-house, except he does speak to me a moment longer than usual; he asks me if I could please iron his light blue shirt. He has never asked me to do more than clean before.

The bigger change occurs the next day. I am squatting on the floor almost inside the cabinet, dusting the glass door, when I see him through it standing in the doorway.

"Sorry," he says. "I wanted to ask you about something, an idea, if you're not too busy, or maybe when you're free. I see you're busy now."

I get up, my legs lengthening. "I am done here." This is going to be the beginning of us being equals, like we always were. I fold my dusting cloth into a neat square and put it on the floor under a chair, and wait for him to join me.

———

Junaid has given me a school exercise book and a pen. He wants me to take notes for him now. He says the City is full of people who are full of ideas for the Town. There is a group that wants to send a truck every month with food, and another that wants to give us their gently used clothes. The students of a university have been collecting books so that the children of the Town grow up literate and have a fair chance in life later on. A team of dentists, psychologists, and pediatricians wants to come over to assess us and give us medicine. I note down everything neatly, and Junaid praises my handwriting and attention to detail. When he arrives the next Monday, he unrolls a large sheet of paper in his office. It is a map, covered with rectangles and squares. "The new school will be here," he says, pointing at a long building next to an empty square. "That is the field for sports. Cricket, volleyball, running." He puts his finger on another shape. "This is the hospital, just an improvement on the existing one. More facilities, larger." Then his finger hops over smaller circles and ovals and arches. "Every town needs beautiful things. We plan to build two fountains. We're going to make a second park, which will have a lot of smaller fountains. These will be lit up at night and the reach of the water will vary in length; we were thinking long, long, short, long, long, short, like that. What do you think?"

I tell him it sounds like a place I would not recognize. He smiles and makes the two of us tea, which we have with biscuits he got from his favorite bakery in the City.

Yesterday, Junaid was on the phone all day finalizing details for a TV crew's visit to the Town to film our situation.

"They will do interviews, Raheela," he said to me, standing up with a groan and stretching his arms over his head. There are no sweat stains in the armpits of his shirt; he is so clean. The last time I washed Masood's few shirts, the armpits had been the color of healthy pale-yellow urine.

"Will they interview me?" I asked, then I thought it sounded as if I wanted to be on TV like a common, gauche small-city person, so I added, in a hard voice, "I don't want to talk to them."

"You can hide in your house with your husband until they're gone." He sounded amused. I did not like that he said I had a husband. I pointedly picked up the jhaaroo and began sweeping to show him my displeasure, but he saw nothing of that and languorously returned to his desk, saying, "Anyway, it will be completely spontaneous, nothing planned."

I did not indicate that I had paid his words much attention; I turned my back to him and tried to look busy. Inside, fear was crawling around in my stomach. I did not like it when he sounded distant, different, better. Later, limbs heavy, I was putting on my things to go home when Junaid came out of his office holding a small cardboard box. "Here," he said. "I know you like namak paaray. From the City." He was standing in his usual slightly stooped way, no longer tall and proud and sure. What I wanted to do was tell him I did not need his food, but I stayed quiet for the sake of Baadal's stomach which must be very empty.

The TV people are a woman with a microphone, a man with a camera, and their driver. They arrive in their van early on Thursday morning at Junaid's office-residence. He introduces me to them as one of the unbreakable, hardworking women of the Town. "Nothing breaks her. Nothing," he says. "She lived through the village drought of the 1970s. And she's living through what seems to be another one. Tough, I tell you." The woman with the microphone asks me five questions. How do I clean myself with dribbles of water? How do I drink? Do I ever fall sick? Do I have brothers and sisters? Did I pass my resilience on to my son? Junaid sits behind his desk, not interfering, while I answer the woman. I am sure I do well; the woman nods frequently. Then she thanks me for my time and the man behind her puts down the camera. Junaid stands up; he is supposed to go with the TV team in their van around the Town. I get up as well, certain that they need someone who knows people here. But Junaid looks at me and says, "I'm going to go back to the City with them afterward. You can head to your home now."

That night I think about the word he had used, *back*, how it had swept down like a blade between us. I am here and he is there and there is nothing I can do about it.

Junaid has brought me a suit from the City. It is a dark red shalwar qameez suit, the color of beetroot. The qameez has a print of small blue diamond shapes. There is also a dupatta made of georgette. When he handed it to me, he said, "It isn't new. It used to be my sister's, but she said it's the wrong size or something and asked if I knew somebody who could use it. And I thought of you, right away." He placed the folded clothes into my hands. "She only wore it once. It's practically new."

I put the clothes on at home. I cook in them and I make Masood's dinner in them. I wait for him to ask me where I got them, but he says nothing. He goes out after dinner and I sit for a long time in front of the TV with the sound very low. When it is almost midnight and he is still not back, I lock the front door and wear my new clothes to bed.

A few days later Masood tells me he is leaving.

"Why?" I ask him.

"There is no one here now to keep staying together for." He speaks quietly.

A sort of panic quickens my heartbeat and makes my stomach hollow. I wonder if he will hold my hands, and I make them available to him, palms up, but he keeps his loosely held in his lap, and after a moment I curl my fingers closed. And then the panic subsides. There was no true fear behind it, I realize; it had merely been the reaction to a big change, not to hurt. It is true what he said; our daughters are dead and our son is far away. I am not hurt.

I ask him where he will live, and he says he knows someone who knows the owner of the old disused soap factory. Masood is going to take one of the empty rooms at the back.

"The owner doesn't mind?"

"It's just a small house falling apart."

"And you have money?" My face becomes warm.

Masood looks away. "Baadal knows."

I cannot help myself. "He talks to you?"

Masood nods.

"I will help you settle in."

"It is just a room, you do not have to come," he says. There is no longing in his words.

"I will bring you food."

"Shaukat is bringing me his brother's single stove there."

"Who is going to look after you if you get sick?"

"There is always someone around. A policeman or a shopkeeper."

The night he leaves, I am on the bed all by myself in a new way. I cry a little, but not out of sadness, only from being very tired. When I go to work the next day I want to tell Junaid what has happened but I am not sure why, so I stay quiet.

2

VISITS

It is when I am standing at my door signing the divorce papers that Masood has brought over that I understand what I am going to do. I am going to ask Junaid to marry me.

I do this the very week that my three months of iddat are over. He is drinking water with loud little gulps and I, holding his washed sheets in my arms, say, "I think the two of us should get married."

He sets down the glass, wipes his mouth with his hand, adjusts his glasses, and looks at me. "Well. I can't say I haven't considered it. It is difficult for a woman to live on her own."

"Yes. Very."

"And it would be a very good example that unusual unions can happen. City-Town. Rich-poor."

"There is no doubt about that."

He smiles, eyes wide, as if the two of us are about to pull a stunt. "Let's do it! Let's set a date!"

A week later, on a hot day in July, we are sitting in a restaurant with plastic covers on tables. We are here for our nikah celebration meal. The owner has made an effort to sweep the floor and dust the windows. Junaid chose this restaurant because it is some way outside the Town but before the City starts. I am wearing a shalwar qameez that my mother had given to me when I had married Masood. The sleeves are edged with lace and there are golden buttons halfway down the front. At the few tables around us are the two witnesses; they are friends of Junaid from his office, men I had not seen before today. His mother could not come because of a flareup of gout in her knees, but his sister is here, sitting at our table. She is quiet and gives me shy smiles. I like her. Junaid brought her over around sunrise this morning; he will drive her back home later.

My son is not here; he must have decided to stay in the City, to keep his distance from me. I had called him on a number that Nabeela reluctantly passed on to me. I didn't know if it was his work number or his home number; I didn't waste time finding out. Baadal only listened as far as the part about Junaid before cutting off the call. But Nabeela and her son Azeem are present. She had shown up at my house to go with me to the one-room office of the qazi where I was to meet Junaid. And now she is sitting at the same table as me and Junaid and his sister. They talk politely about the humidity, the traffic. My sister gives my husband a present of a new watch and his sister a shawl. It is odd that this has to be done in a restaurant. At Masood's time the presents were given inside my house, with his aging parents on one sofa and mine on another. I am not comparing; I am merely remembering.

An hour ago, in the qazi's office, my head had felt heavy for a moment as I held the pen, but I signed the papers quickly, without lingering. It becomes heavy again when I see my sister eating her food quietly. Is she, like me, wondering if Aneela is above the ground or under it? Is she remembering the silly fight Suhail and I once had over a pen?

❧

Junaid's car has an air conditioner but it does not work very well and the air coming out of the vents is only slightly cool. The red lipstick on my mouth feels sticky. He is taking me to the City for our honeymoon. We are to stay the first two nights at his mother's house and the third and final night at a hotel. In the car he reminds me that it is the duty of families to maintain good relations, so I must be sure to ask his mother about her health and his sister about how she spends her time. I say, "Yes, it is" and "Yes, I will" while I think, *Does Baadal know that I will be there? Will I see him?*

Junaid says, "Now, don't make a fuss about your son when we go to your sister's house. I don't like scenes. He is an adult. He will meet you if he wants to. I want us to have a nice little holiday."

I wait a full minute before speaking. "I have never fussed about my son." I turn my face toward the window, away from him. With my thumb, I wipe the red off my lips.

When we reach the City, he starts pointing at signs painted on walls, at the shapes of buildings, the billboards on the roadsides. I find the buildings uninteresting, boxy, and brown, the ads large and unrefined. This is not like the journey I had taken all those years ago with my Baba and Ammi and Nabeela. But for Junaid, after so many days in the Town, the City is a fresh revelation; he leans forward eagerly while I press myself into my seat.

Suddenly, he swerves the car onto the dirt, next to a group of fruit sellers' carts. He pulls up the handbrake, opens his door, and leaps out, pushing it shut while loudly greeting a man standing behind a mound of green grapes. The man grins and asks him if his missus wouldn't like some fruit? Junaid says something to him and they both laugh. Then the seller gives him a small bulging bag. The car door opens and Junaid leaps back in, tossing the bag onto my lap. He starts the engine and says, "So much variety here. So damn much."

The house his mother and sister live in is smaller than how I remember Hamid's house to be, a single-story structure shaped like a box. There are flowers in pots right outside the main walls with a fence of bricks in front of them and a shiny black rectangle sign under the bell that says, in white letters, Aslam Villa, B/76. His mother greets me politely, as if I am a neighbor. His sister gives me a hug and is more generous with her smiles. In the little sitting room, I give them two sets of unstitched cloth that Junaid had bought on my behalf and said would make nice presents from me to them.

His sister, whose name is Fazeela, says, "Raheela bhabhi, thank you so much. You should come with me to the tailor tomorrow please."

I tell her I would like to do that, then ask about her days. I ask Junaid's mother about her health. Fazeela gets up to start laying the table and I do the same, suddenly nervous about having to talk about my mother or father or, worse, my son.

"Please, you must be tired," the sister implores.

"Please, it is no trouble at all."

There are seven dishes that Fazeela and I set out: fish covered in green masala, chicken karahi, matar pulao, salad, chana daal, gobi saalan, and raita. I have never before had such a variety of food on a table that is immediately accessible to me, not even at my first wedding. After this there is dessert, two kinds of it: kheer and sooji halwa. Junaid eats from every dish and platter, seconds and thirds even. I am revolted by the fish and do not like the kheer but force myself to swallow both. All three of them keep on eating, their talk moves away from me and on to relatives and friends and situations I don't know about. I see them and hear them, and I don't understand what I am doing here. When we are done I take the plates, now strewn with small bones and streaks of saalan, back into the kitchen, and stand there for a moment. Where are all the people I used to know? But it is a thought I have to train myself not to indulge in, so I walk to the drawing room and pick up my cup of tea.

In the morning Junaid takes his sister to the tailor and I go along. When he steps out of the car to buy milk, she tells me her brother is a very kind and attentive person. "Do you have any brothers?" she asks.

"No," I say.

Afterward, Junaid asks her to help me buy new clothes. "The only good suit I have seen you wear is your wedding one, and you can't wear that forever," he says to me. It is what I am wearing right now.

In the afternoon, Junaid and I visit my sister. He whistles when he sees the address I have written down.

"What does her husband do?" he asks.

"Her husband is dead. He used to work in a bank."

What will I say to Baadal if I see him? If? Why if?

My sister's son Karim and his wife Asma are home with her. Their two young children look in on us shyly then run away. When Asma sits down I wonder if she is expecting a third one. There are vases with flowers standing on corner tables. Against one wall is a polished wooden cabinet with a tray of glasses and jugs of water. The floor is covered with a soft gray carpet. Everything gleams, everything is comfortable.

The last time I came to my sister's house was four years ago, when her husband passed away. It was also the first time I had been to her home. Baadal and Masood were with me. How spacious, I had thought, the women in the living room and the men in the drawing room. A baby started to cry. The mother asked, "Where can I change my baby?" and a maid took her upstairs. A room for every need, I thought. I remember Nabeela's eyes had been swollen with crying; there was not a particle of makeup on her face. Sitting on a chair, with the light from the sun coming in through the soft white curtains, she looked lovely. Even grief couldn't be ugly in a house such as this one. Even I was made to feel softer, gentler, in those moments that we stood together, my nephews and Asma, my son and my husband. We were a tight knot of family in a beautiful place, gathered for a loved one's funeral.

In the kitchen, Nabeela asks me if I am happy and I say yes, I think so.

"Is Baadal coming?" I ask casually.

"He told Karim he has a lot of work," she answers the same way. "He is doing well. He and Meena seem well."

"Tell me where they live. Please."

She hesitates for a second, then tears a page out of a magazine and writes down my son's address. I fold it and put it inside my handbag.

The hotel Junaid has chosen is a narrow ten-story building sandwiched between a bank and another hotel. It is called Royal Inn. "This is the lobby," he tells me. There is a polished marble counter here and a man behind it wearing a badge with the name Naseem on it. In the village, my mother had a friend called Naseem, an old woman whose face I was frightened of when she used to visit us. I think, how strange that a man has an old woman's name, but then I have never heard of anyone in the City named the way we named our children in the Town. I wander around the small area while Junaid speaks to the man. The walls have red and brown stripes adorned with small dark brown flowers. I touch them and feel paper. The big light hanging from the ceiling is called a chandelier, I remember. There had been one like it in Hamid's house; even the diamond-shaped structures are the same, throwing the yellow light among themselves and onto us.

"We could have gone to a cheaper hotel," I tell Junaid later. "That chandelier downstairs is so expensive."

He gives a short laugh. "Glass and metal? Hardly. If we don't order anything from the hotel restaurant, it's just a hundred rupees a night." There is pride and frugality at the same time in his voice.

Later, we eat at a small restaurant in a shopping plaza. My stomach starts rumbling almost as soon as we step out of it.

"I need to go to the bathroom," I tell Junaid.

"We'll be at the hotel in a couple of hours."

"I'm not feeling well." There is cold sweat all over my face. I breathe shallowly to keep the nausea away.

Junaid sighs. "All right, I'll take you back. Our last day in the City and you had to get sick. I don't think we'll come back again any time soon, so it's too bad we'll miss the dry fruit market and the marble bazaar."

At the front of the hotel he asks if I can manage going up by myself, he might as well do a few errands now that he has extra time. I nod and get out of the car. The man at the front desk hands me my key and looks at me curiously. I am afraid that the movement of the elevator will make me feel worse so I climb the stairs, slowly with pauses. When I finally reach my room, I let myself in and, with gratitude and sickness running through me, I lock the door.

For the next few hours I move in a haze among the toilet, the sink, and the stretch of carpet outside the bathroom. At some point I bring a pillow and the blanket from the bed. I doze off. I wake up. I vomit. I stumble to the toilet. I clean myself, then lie down again on my soft pillow under the warm blanket, hoping desperately that this was the last resurgence.

When Junaid knocks, I adjust my clothes and shut the bathroom door. I return the pillow and blanket back onto the bed. All this tires me out. I let him in, and the smell of food hits me.

"I brought us dinner," he announces. "How are you feeling? Any better?"

I make slight movements with my head. I wish he would leave. I wish I could be alone again for a few hours more. Maybe forever. But he is here in the room, setting out containers of rice and what smells like chicken curry, talking loudly about something he saw and laughing. He turns on the small TV. I groan and lie on the bed, my back to the smells and the sounds. I feel a hand on my forehead.

"No fever," I hear him say. "Looks like food poisoning. Rest is the only cure."

He lowers the TV volume and sets a glass of water by me. When I go to the bathroom again I do not feel too embarrassed, but I keep the water running in the sink the whole time.

The next morning is our last one in the City. I have been feeling better, and Junaid has been kind and attentive, so when he asks if I am able to go out for a little sightseeing before we head back, I say yes. He drives us all the way to the sea. He is in a very good mood. He playfully suggests that I go on a camel ride, and I smile and decline. He buys me roasted corn, warm from the sand in a vendor's cart. "That's good, right?" He sighs and moves his arms expansively, from the apartments standing far away to the sea in front of us. "You'll be surprised how great this City is." He walks to the water's edge one last time. I check to see if the paper with Baadal's address is still inside the small pocket in my handbag. When Junaid comes back, we start the journey back home.

☙

When Junaid works he shuts the door of his office, leaving me by myself in the kitchen, the bedroom, and the living room. "Why don't you go to the market," he suggests, standing in the doorway, one hand on the handle, rocking on his heels, radiating impatience to get on with his papers and his phone calls and his stamps.

"Do you want me to take notes?" I ask.

"No, no, I've got everything under control. But thank you. Maybe you can buy me some peanuts when you're out."

Sometimes he asks me to watch the news with him. He points his thick forefinger at a new shopping complex on the screen. "Now sit and learn," he says excitedly, swinging his feet off the table and onto the floor, leaning forward. "That developer making all that? They are interested in building a shopping arcade here on the outskirts of the Town. I told them about the government's water scheme for the Town, and that row of houses being built—better-quality construction, new school right there—and the developers said they were on board. On board!"

One day, he gives me a project. He hands me a long list of names, running over both sides of a sheet of paper. "These are doctors who have expressed an interest in visiting the Town," he says. "You have to call them and find out who can come next month."

"What kind of doctors?" I ask him.

"Pediatricians, women's doctors, eye doctors, a psychologist."

"What will the psychologist do?"

"I think she wants to see what living here does to people," Junaid says in an offhand manner.

"Will she evaluate you?"

"Most certainly. In fact, I will be a special case study, being a person who lives in the City *and* the Town."

When Junaid takes a break for lunch, I use the phone and call the doctors. I make checkmarks and question marks against names. I tuck the receiver under my chin and reach for my notebook; it feels good that I need it. The calls take me one whole afternoon. In the end my fingers ache from holding the receiver but I want to do more.

I start writing down names of places where the doctors can meet the Townspeople. The unused secondary school building, the clinic, the marketplace. I begin to draw a picture of the school, placing the doctors in different rooms. In my mind there is a line of people going around the building. Chacha Ameer for his eyes, Masood for his ears, a child from my old street who had stopped growing last year. I give Junaid my notes and the list of doctors. He takes them happily and says thank you, he will look into them.

This is a good reason to call Baadal; he could visit here for free checkups. Meena too. I could get them to be first in all the lines. I pick up the receiver but self-consciousness overwhelms me. Junaid could listen to me talk in that formal, stilted way that my son and I have, and what would he think then? How strange this mother is with her son.

❧

Junaid makes me false promises now. He puts on the shoes he likes to wear to the City and says to me that he will be back in two days, or three days, or four days. Then, on the evening he is to come back, I get a phone call from him. He says it will take him two more days, maybe four.

"What do you need to go so often for?" I ask him as we eat a rare dinner together.

"For the big doctors' visit that I am trying to arrange, of course." He clicks his tongue. "You know, the doctors that the people in your Town need so desperately? Don't you want to see them improving?"

The next time he comes out of the bathroom smelling of shaving foam and cologne and stands in front of the mirror, tilts his head, carefully parts his hair, and takes out his good shoes, I say, "I don't want you to go."

"What are you accusing me of?" His hands pause in the middle of pulling his sock over his foot. "I don't have another woman in the City, if that's what you're afraid of."

"I don't think that. I didn't say that."

"No, but you think it." His feet done, he buttons his cuffs.

"You're hardly ever here anymore."

"I will tell my associates to stop this doctors' project because my wife is bored." He speaks levelly, politely, mockingly. "Is that all right? I will stop the good work this Town needs, let the suicide rate get higher, because you are jealous, because your mind stops at the walls of your very small imagination."

I sit for a while in the slight disturbance created in the air by the shutting of the door, then get up and go to my old house.

3

HOUSES

DUST COVERS EVERYTHING INSIDE. The netting over the window in my bedroom has come off the edges. My first afternoon there, I remove cobwebs and wipe surfaces. In the evening, I wash the few plates and glasses in the kitchen; they have not been touched in a long time. I go into Baadal's room last. The only things in his cupboard are his school shirt and trousers. On the floor under his bed is a T-shirt with a large rip in the neckline. His books and papers are on the chipped brown table. What was his last day at school? I cannot remember. There is nothing else in the room that can definitively say he used to study and sleep there. I use the inch tape I have taken from Junaid's house and write down the height and width of the windows. I measure the floor and the bed, the doorframe, the little table. I reach for the switch to turn off the bulb but at that moment it flickers and dies. I return to the office-residence, Junaid's home, but I do so reluctantly. It is not because he is not there; I look forward to his absences. I drag my feet because I am fighting against my desire to sleep in my own house. I am trying to stay with this new husband of mine, even if he is not there.

———

It is only when the days start growing shorter that I start lying down on my old bed. I had expected to be sad, when I first stretched out on it slowly, but I didn't feel much. Many afternoons later, when this way of resting has become a habit, an old memory starts sneaking into my brain, of having my face held and kissed, arms around my middle. I don't know whose lips and whose arms; that is irrelevant. And then another memory pushes this one to the side, that of the evening I followed Masood to the well and asked him to come home. He told me to go away, I was interrupting his work. I lunged forward and wrested the shovel from him. He looked at the men, who had stepped back, and he laughed. He had never laughed at me before. I swung the shovel, the devil giving me the energy to lift it and move it through the air. The handle struck Masood's legs. I turned to run and a clod of dirt hit me, and then another. Masood screamed names at me. But these particular pictures in my head appear farther and farther apart, and when they come I get off the bed and prepare a cup of tea and drink it, the entire act pulling a curtain across my small, unsolvable lonelinesses.

I see a boy in my dream one afternoon. The dream is a brief one. When the boy sees me, he says his name; he says, "It's me, Suhail," and I am sad and worried because I do not completely recognize him. Still, I keep looking at him and he lets me, until I begin to see that the forehead and the nose and the eyes are like the ones my brother used to have. And because he now knows that I know him, he tells me he is so happy where he is and I shouldn't worry. Then he reaches out his hands and they touch a wall. And then he is gone. This is how I know that I have to dig a well.

The shovel has been at the back of the house since Masood left it there. There is still dirt on the handle and the blade. On the other side of the house, the grass burnt out a long time ago. Small rocks accumulate underfoot. I squat over the ground, pick up the rocks, and throw them into a pile. I try to work fast, before the sun starts to bake my body, but the rocks don't seem to end. When there is enough clear, I decide it is time to dig. I tie an end of my dupatta around my head, the rest of it trailing down my back. The first inch or so of the earth is dry and yields to the blade, but below that it starts to feel packed. Over and over, I push in the shovel and bring out the soil. My throat and tongue become parched and my ears throb. The shovel falls to the ground. I crawl to where there is no sun. It feels so good to lie down with my eyes closed that I wish to give in completely and faint. For a few minutes I hover between complete darkness and daylight before, finally, drifting away.

Someone is calling me—"Oye, Baadal's mother, office-residency woman"—and I open my eyes. For a moment, I do not know who this woman is, sitting by my feet on the ground, and I am gripped with fear that I have tempted an old ghost into my house. Then I remember; she is the mother of Baadal's friend Juman, and her name is Aleena.

She came because she had heard moaning from outside the wall. She knew I was there. She came because she thought I was in need of help. That is the most that she speaks in consecutive breaths for the rest of that afternoon. While I sit on the sofa and rest a little longer, she sits on the other chair, her hands in her lap, staring a little to the side of the blank screen. The expression on her face is not one of resignation, just of waiting. When I get up and start putting away things here and there, she doesn't say, "Let me," just gets up and does the thing next in line. We eat what's left in the fridge from Junaid's house. At nine o'clock, I tell her, "Well. I am going to sleep now," and she says, "I will sleep on the sofa," and we say goodnight.

One morning a few weeks later, when Aleena is gone, I find I cannot stay inside the house. I try to dig the well, but the windows keep looking at me. I decide to visit Masood. When I think about how long it has been since I last saw him, it makes me dizzy.

I walk through the gates of the soap factory, toward his room, past the desolate building, and the excitement I had been feeling gives way to sadness. Then he sees me and smiles in the way that people who have known each other a very long time do, and I feel all right again. We sit on plastic chairs outside his room. He makes me a cup of tea, asks cordially after my health. He does not ask about Junaid. I tell him that Baadal and Meena are not living at my sister's house anymore and that Baadal has a steady job, and he and his wife are happy. My voice is falsely cheery but then I blurt out, "He will still not talk to me."

"He will, when he is ready."

I understand then that he already knew everything I just told him. My heart beats in a painful way as I sit on the chair, holding my cup. After a while, it becomes possible to speak normally again. I say, as if merely inquiring after an acquaintance, "I wonder what he does, what he likes to eat now."

I have worked out the problem of the old cushions in the living room where Baadal, his father, and I used to sit. Among the clothes that I don't wear anymore, have not put on in years, are two very large dupattas, one blue and the other green. I am going to use them to make new covers. I start my work at night after Junaid has gone to sleep, but I make sure to go to bed no later than midnight; I don't want to look tired the next day. I have also scrubbed the fridge and left it on; I think it works well. I wish I could paint the walls a fresh new color, pale yellow or maybe cream, but I do not have the money for that. I plan to wash them with detergent.

I take a small pot of rice and daal to Masood and tell him that I do not know if I should wait for Baadal to call me or if I should contact him myself again.

"Nabeela refuses to help," I complain. "She says this is between me and him."

"She's not wrong, really. She hardly knows anything about the situation. There's no salt in this."

I hand him the salt. "The phone needs fixing again."

"I'll send someone tomorrow."

In the evening, in my house, I dial Baadal's number. I have practiced what I will say to him. "Come see the house! You and Meena can live here anytime you like." The bell starts ringing and I quickly set the receiver down. I cannot invite him and his wife over, the lawn is not ready yet. The house smells clean and there is water in the tank and the pipes. My sewing has not been very good but the cushions make the living room look brighter.

Aleena and I go to the new plant nursery in the Town. I go there and buy a bag of fertilizer. I pay for it out of the money Junaid leaves me for groceries. From his garden, I snip off a few zinnias. He recently paid a gardener to have the flowerbed remade, since the Town has now been given a larger allotment of water. I save seeds from tomatoes and chilis, and I take all of this back to my old home and sow it into the layer of soil and fertilizer.

A dream I have a few days later is that Baadal and Masood are digging under a strong lamplight held up by somebody I cannot see. They find patches of grass in a layer of soil. My sister Aneela is sitting at the bottom of the vertical dirt tunnel, eating the grass. I wake up with a sour flavor in my mouth.

❧

Masood has a table now, sourced by Kawsar, he tells me. I set down a bowl of khichri on it. The air is chilly and it comforts me to see Masood in a thick, beige sweater. I wonder who gave it to him.

In the middle of a sentence his words start to slur, and slowly his head and shoulders bend forward until his face comes to rest on his plate, in the food. I let out a garbled noise, a mixture of a loud gasp and words. I pull the plate out from under him, leaving rice and daal smeared on his cheek. His eyes open slightly, all white, before closing again. But he is still breathing; my fingers on his wrist feel a slow pulse.

There are words coming out from my mouth, prayers and Baadal's name, as I run to the tin-roofed room nearby where there is a phone. I hold the receiver but cannot remember my son's number or the doctor's and I realize I have never known the hospital's number. So I call my own house, and Juman's mother answers.

When I hear footsteps and people talking, my heart leaps, I am sure it is Baadal. But it is Kawsar and the doctor. Of course. How foolish of me to forget that my son lives far away. I explain to the doctor what happened and he nods in sharp little movements, the corners of his mouth turned down as if weary. He keeps his eyes on his shoes or on Masood, never looking at me. He tells me to wait outside the room. But suddenly I am angry that I had to drag Masood into the room and onto his bed all by myself. I am exhausted by being alone. I do not want to be dismissed. "You can go ahead and check him," I snap.

The doctor shakes his head and puts a stethoscope on Masood's chest. "Wake up, come on," he says. He removes the stethoscope, straps a black cuff around an inert arm, and pumps a gray bulb. He takes off the cuff, prepares an injection, and pushes the needle into the other arm. "Come on, wake up." Masood's mouth opens with a low sound, then his eyelids lift a little. The doctor puts away his instruments and writes on a pad. "High blood pressure," he says to Kawsar, tearing off a leaf. "I have given him an injection. These are his medicines. Two times a day, both of them with meal." Taking long strides, he leaves. All of this happens in barely fifteen minutes.

Kawsar takes a spot in the corner and falls asleep. Masood falls asleep. I bring my knees up and rest my chin between them. Baadal will come, I am sure. Will he bring Meena with him? Will he speak to me? What will I say to his wife?

It is nighttime when he comes through the door. I rise quickly, wanting to touch his face and squeeze his hands, and for a moment he looks at me as if irresolute, then walks to his father's side. No one else enters. I speak before Kawsar can.

"Your father has high blood pressure."

Kawsar passes him the prescription.

"He is going to be okay," I go on.

It is ridiculous that I feel so nervous. I make myself speak again.

"How is Meena?"

"She is fine. You both can go home now, get some food and rest. I'll stay here."

I understand that his comfort is in my leaving, so I do as he says. Outside the factory I give Kawsar some money and ask him to buy dinner for Baadal. These are the only things I can offer, my absence and food. When I see him again I want him to sit by me or let me sit by him. I want to explain to him about Junaid, why I married him and why, now, I am living in my own house again. But he does not give me a chance to talk to him alone, away from Masood.

I come by every day to bring Masood food. On Friday, as I am leaving, Baadal appears in the distance, and I stop. He gets closer to the factory gate and I stand very still, eyes moving from his combed hair to his clean shoes. If he sees me he might go back, or he might go on and meet his father in a bad mood. So I turn toward the longer way home. When I feel braver, I stay there a moment longer and silently will him to wave to me. Maybe he knows this because he keeps his head down as he walks.

For weeks, we come and go like this, as autumn turns to winter. I keep myself busy between Baadal's visits. There is always something to do at my house, the floor to sweep and the furniture to be dusted and the cobwebs to be removed. I dig the well a little deeper. One time I go to Junaid's house and take a packet of raw chicken from the freezer and put it into my handbag. I stop to use the bathroom and see new soap there. I collect that too. I cook the meat at my own house then take it to Masood, imagining Baadal would eat it as well. And when I see Baadal's father, his head wrapped in my shawl, his thin body under two blankets, I tell him about the plants in the lawn. I don't tell him about the well; I am planning it to be a surprise.

I talk and talk even as Masood's eyes close and he slips away into medicated rest: this is where we will sit and this is where we will stand; Meena and I will talk about cooking or cleaning—are the potatoes peeled, has the washing been brought inside—and maybe she is the kind of person who likes to keep herself busy mending clothes so I will bring her a collection of things with small holes in them; and if I cannot find anything, I will make tears into a few edges and sleeves and save them for her; and in the evening you, Baadal's father, will be on the sofa and Meena will bring in the tea; and, a short while later, there will be a knock on the door and it will be Baadal with biscuits from the bakery, and he will sit on the chair by the low table.

MEENA

1

FIRST LESSONS

I WAS NAMED by my mother in a fit of anger. I was almost seven weeks old and my *dada* had still not decided what I should be called. My mother marched to the old man's room on the upper floor and announced that her baby was going to be called Meena.

"I read the name in a magazine. A *film* magazine," she had added with relish.

"You are not going to name a child of this family after an amoral character," my grandfather said.

"That amoral character gives part of her earnings to an orphanage. I think she is perfectly lovely."

My grandfather, who did not talk to his daughter-in-law much after that incident, told his granddaughter, me, that the woman in the magazine was a bad sort of woman who had been left all alone in the end.

"What did she do?" I asked him.

"She did not listen to her father, and later, she did not listen to her husband."

When my mother wasn't around, my *dada* insisted on calling me by the name Izzat, or honor.

Sometime between the age of six and seven, my father returned home with another wife. He lived with her in a room upstairs. From around corners, I observed her; this woman did not raise her voice, and she made sure that water was served first to her husband, then her father-in-law, and lastly, herself. My grandfather made her feel welcome and built her a separate living room and small kitchen. I, who had all the loyalty for my mother and none for my father, helped her tie up his clothes and shoes in an old bedsheet and throw the bundle into a stream.

ᏉᏅ

I know the story of how my mother and father got married. I know it because I asked her once. She told me that when she was a young girl she had gone to see a wise man. The wise man sat behind a screen and told her that she was going to have a lot of children because the man she was destined to marry was a good person. In the court-yard where this man sat were a lot of other women waiting to consult about their futures. A bareheaded and bare-armed woman with a fat braid and a gold nose pin walked around, collecting payment.

My mother met my father not long after that. She was at a well, pulling on the rope to bring up the pail when this man stepped up and silently took over the rope. In a few quick, strong movements, he hauled out the half-full pail and emptied it into the pot by her feet. My mother told me she had smiled at him then, a quick, daring smile, and memorized his face. Broad forehead, light brown skin, lips that were not thin nor full. She wasn't embarrassed when talking about my father like that with me; it was as if she were talking about someone else. She found out his name and his circumstances. A father and a farm. His brothers and sisters had either died or moved far away.

One evening, she visited his house all by herself. When he opened the door she almost forgot the action she had practiced by herself, but only for a moment. She gave him a piece of paper. On it, she had written her proposal of marriage, and brief facts about herself: no mother, no father, and currently lodging on a mattress at the back of the house where she worked. Two days later, my father sent his answer: yes.

❦

When I was sixteen, I met a man who was kind. Talib came from a village almost a hundred kilometers to the east. He made me forget about my father and about most bad things. Sometimes, when I was sure my mother was busy for a long time, I stood in front of the tall, narrow mirror propped against a wall in our room. The skin over my knees and elbows was dry. My torso melted into my hips with barely a curve. My chest, like my stomach, was almost flat. Somewhere in there, my body, despite the scattered meals and the bad water which made me lose those meals, could make babies for Talib.

He told my mother he wanted to marry me. She said if I did that my *dada* would throw her out and have me brought back home. After spending some days praying and thinking, she told me she knew how she could help us. She kept watch one night so I could slip out of the front door. Wrapped around me was her largest chaadar. The only time I cried was when I felt the hard little knob of money she had tied up in a corner of it.

Talib and I moved along the river, living on whatever we earned. He tried to find work on farms, and I cleaned homes or sewed or helped look after babies. But the rainfall had not been enough for some time, and farmers were closing down their small plots of land and selling most of their animals to buyers who came from the City. For almost two years, Talib and I kept on this way. Our difficulties were made less complicated by the fact that I loved him and he loved me. It got harder, though, when he got ill with dysentery. The nearest doctor was half a day away. I went to the wife of a man who owned a bull cart. I told her I thought I was going to have a baby and needed to see the doctor. Could they lend me and my husband the bull and the cart in exchange for me doing their housework without money for two weeks? The wife went inside to ask her husband, and came back with a yes.

"If you work for a month, though," she added, looking at me with her head tilted.

"All right," I said.

I spread all of our sheets over the cart and settled Talib over them with a pillow and a blanket. He protested that this was not the right thing to do, he should be the one taking care of me. I sat in the driver's seat and, heart beating fast, I took the reins in my hands. It was around three in the morning, earlier than anyone usually woke up. I did not want us to be seen. I drove along the track that led out of the village. From the back, Talib asked me a few times if I was all right. Then he fell asleep. In the quiet, with the motion of the wheels over the mud and the steady movement of the animals' legs, my nervousness settled down like a thin layer of pressed clay; it was there but not dominantly so. I stopped a few times to get a little food and water into my husband, or when he needed to defecate or vomit.

The clinic was a small building. I got off the cart, my back and arms stiff, apprehension rising again. I held Talib's hand and went in through the single door, people parting to let us through. There was a narrow hallway with a bench on each side. The weakest of men sat on those, or women with children. I grabbed the sleeve of a man in a shirt and pants, holding a pen and a clipboard.

"My husband is very sick," I said, mouth dry, underarms sweaty. "We need to see the doctor right away."

"Name?" the man asked.

"Talib Mian."

"Take a seat. We will call you." He began to move away.

"We have come from very far."

"Bibi, everyone here has come from very far. Everyone must wait for their turn."

We went into the courtyard. There was only one area of shade, provided by a single tree. Patients and their families had already claimed that space; they returned my glances with immovability. Talib and I sat against a wall, the sun at an angle on our backs. He fell asleep with his head on my shoulder. After some time, I thought I felt him shiver. I took off my dupatta and spread it over him, looking up anxiously to see if the man with the clipboard would call us next. But then I dozed off too, waking up with a start, confused and aching. When I remembered everything, I turned toward Talib; he was moaning and his body was shaking. The sun had moved away. I scrambled up and ran into the building. When the clipboard man saw me, he held up his hands placatingly even before I opened my mouth.

"Now!" I spoke anyway. "We need the doctor now. It has been too long!"

The man nodded as if he had been meaning to invite us in all along. "The doctor is ready for him."

It was difficult to get Talib to walk. I had to ask for help. Talib's limbs started jerking as men took him into the doctor's room. They told me to wait outside, and when I stayed standing, well-meaning women held my arms and gently pulled me onto a bench. An hour later, I found out that my husband had died of a seizure.

They buried him in a cemetery nearby later that day. One of the women from the clinic took me home, fed me, and gave me her own bed to sleep in. In the morning, I got onto the seat of the bull cart. I thought about going back to my mother, but that home was an earlier part of my life, and a long distance away in time and kilometers.

Besides, I had things to return.

For a few months, I lived by myself in the little mud house Talib and I had put together. Some of the men and women, when they saw me, said my husband was out of pain now. Nobody asked me about my pretend baby. The wife of the bull cart man felt sorry for me and said I only had to do her housework for two weeks and not the full month. After that, I got taken on by a family with a very old woman and a new baby. My duties included taking the old woman to the bathroom and giving her food, and looking after the baby when his mother was not nursing him. The husband and wife could not give me steady money, only a little of their own food and some cash when they could spare it, but that was fine with me.

Once, I saw the husband watching me as I worked. I drew my dupatta around me, making sure my outline was indistinct and no inch of skin showed. That evening, I was walking to my home when I heard someone running behind me. It was the man. He held out something wrapped in a newspaper.

"You forgot this," he said.

"Thank you." I took the package. It felt oily. In my state of alertness, I could not remember if it was really mine or if he was pretending, but I did not want to linger.

I waited until I was home before unwrapping the newspaper. Inside it was a puri with a ball of halwa in its center. The man had given me a present. I ate a little bit that night, saving the rest for the next day's breakfast. I thought about the tall, thin man who lived in the house I worked in, and for a while I felt very lonely. I curled up on my mat on the floor, my forehead almost touching my knees.

It would be so easy to have him. I prayed very hard that I wouldn't.

☙

The woman at the center showed me which needle worked best on the thick cotton of the tops of shoes. She laid out a pencil and the threads, blue, yellow, green.

"Remember to always sketch first," she said. "It cannot be untidy just because it's handmade."

I nodded and picked up my pencil. On the beige cloth, I copied the pattern taped to my table. A small bouquet of three flowers and three leaves. The rules for the color choices were simple; the flowers could not all be blue or yellow; green was only for the leaves. This was my ninth day at work, and every morning the woman in charge gave me the same instructions. There were other women at tables throughout the room. A few, like me, were widows. All of us were good with a needle and thread.

When I had arrived here, I meant to stop for only a few nights before going on to the Town I had heard about. I was going to ask a woman for food in return for doing her chores; I had become good at getting by like that. Sometimes, they offered me space on their floor for a few nights. I only accepted if the woman was a widow. A few times, I had not been able to find shelter, and I had sat up all night against the wall of whatever religious structure I could find. In this village, there was a kind widow who had got me the job at the Local Crafts Center.

The arrangement for the workers there was that the women were given lodging, if they needed it, and money. The rooms on the ground floor were where we worked, the rooms above were where we could live. There were actual beds there, donated by an industrialist's wife from a nearby city. I enjoyed the luxury of a proper mattress.

On the twelfth day, I got a visit from the kind widow. She had found me a man. He had his own successful furniture store in the City and a house in the Town. The widow even had a photograph of him. He was standing in front of a tree, arms crossed, half smile on his face.

"Has he seen me?" I asked, confused.

"Here and there," the widow said, smiling. "He will be happy if you agree. He told me he doesn't want any dowry."

"I don't know how to have him meet my mother."

The widow held up a hand and tilted her head and pressed her lips lightly. "I've told him your parents have passed away."

"I've been married before."

"And he knows that, child. But tell him again yourself, afterward. It sets a wife on the right tone with the husband, when she lets him know things about herself."

I remembered the man who had brought me food in secret, out of sight of his wife, and said to the widow to say yes to the furniture man.

∽

Another story that I know from my mother is of how she and I had run away from a fire. I was six. My parents had had a bad year with the crops on their little plot of land, the narrow canals had dried up, and we had no money. My father had always barricaded our door at night, passing an iron rod across the width of it over little a loop at either end. He had nailed those into place himself. When I asked him why he did that he said it was to make sure wild animals didn't break down our old door. After the failure with the crops, my father began getting us inside and putting the rod in place earlier than sundown. When the landlord sent his men to collect the rent, my father told them he will have the money in a week or two. When the men hammered on the door with their fists, he refused to open it.

I have a few pieces in my mind of what happened next. I remember waking up to the sound of shattered glass and seeing a ball of fire on the floor, a few inches away from the ends of our mattresses.

I remember shouts and the smell of smoke. When telling me this story, my mother added proudly that I didn't cry, not even when she dragged me outside, away from my beloved doll, and not even when I saw the flames spreading over our little piece of land. My mother set me down while she and my father tried to put out the fire with the four buckets of water they had saved. This I remember vividly: the flames creeping along slowly, little orange, faceless bodies as tall as my fingers. My mother said she picked me up and ran. Sometimes she carried me, flopped over her shoulder like a bag. Sometimes she held my hand tight in hers and we walked. I don't remember being hungry but my mother said she would have chosen my crying over my complaining about my empty stomach. Days after that night with the fire, she moved to the house that I spent the rest of my childhood in. It was where my father and grandfather finally found us. My mother said she had been so happy to see my father.

"And that's when he started to change," I added.

"Yes. That is when it all started to become different," she concluded.

ဆ

The furniture man brought me to his home in the Town the afternoon of the day we got married. He gave me gifts. A thin gold bracelet, a gold necklace, a pair of gold earrings, a blue sari which he said would go beautifully with my dark skin. There was also a set of makeup brushes, and blush and face powders in shiny little black boxes. He told me to stay in my red shalwar qameez all day long. "You don't have to clean or cook today," he assured me. So I stayed dressed up, and he went out sometime around four in the afternoon and came back at ten. He shook me awake and we ate the biryani and kheer he had brought. When he finished eating, he said let's go to the bedroom. He kept the light off and waited for me. I said, "I have been married before." He said that did not matter to him, it did not lessen my value in his eyes.

He was not rough, but he was quick. He fell asleep at once. Quietly, I took a shower, prayed Isha, and lay awake as long as I could, afraid that I would see Talib in a dream and say his name out loud.

I knew I had to be a different kind of wife now; my new husband was just a different person. I learned the way he liked his tea and his egg. When he was in the mood to talk, I listened. Otherwise I didn't offer much of my thoughts. He seemed, for the most part, indifferent to my state. He did not ask why I looked tired or if my feet ached or if I wanted company. He did not ask me what I did all day long. He did not explain his hours of coming and going; he seemed to consider himself unanswerable to me. He ate if he was hungry, or just changed his clothes and went to sleep. If he was in the mood he asked me to come to bed, but that happened less and less. Sometimes I would lay next to him and put his arm over me, just to be touched a little, and wait to see if he would wake up, but he would keep on snoring.

Still, I asked him one day to show me his furniture store, and he did take me to see it. It was not in the City but a little outside the Town. It was a lot smaller than I had imagined it. What space was inside was almost entirely taken up by a two-seater sofa with an ugly scroll design along the headrest, two tables, some lamps, rolls of carpets like columns along a wall, and a bed with a shiny brown blanket. It was very warm inside, and dark, and there was a man at the back, next to a tall cupboard, who stared at me while my husband told me where the different pieces had come from.

When he spotted the man, he said, "Ah, good you're here. Meet your *bhabi*." The man took a step forward, put his hand on his chest, and said welcome, and congratulations, and would I like a cold drink or a cup of tea? I said I wasn't thirsty. Then he said, "Would *bhabi* like something to eat, maybe? I can run to the market and get some samosa." I refused again, said I was not hungry, and thanked him for his hospitality. Outside the shop my husband and I walked to the car. I waited for him to unlock it, but he handed me some money and said there were rickshaws at the end of the street. I was angry, but later, when he came home, he was angrier. He slammed the door shut and sat on the sofa, his face pale, a cigarette in his fingers. I fixed my gaze upon its orange tip.

"What was that behavior, Meena?" His voice was vibrating.

"What behavior?"

"That was my friend in the store, and you talked down to him. Do you have any idea how much you embarrassed me today?"

"I was polite, I just didn't feel like eating or drinking."

"When a host offers a guest something, the correct thing to do is to accept it, do you understand?"

I took a step back, and he stood up.

"You know what he said to me? He said, 'I think I offended *bhabi*. Please ask her to forgive me.' Are you, a pathetic woman I picked out of a mass of pathetic women, someone to apologize to?"

I said, "Well, yes, he was staring at me the whole time."

My husband moved. I ran into the room, but he was quicker, and grabbed me by my hair and dragged me out, into the living room again. He forced me onto the floor, and after that I stopped thinking, stopped listening, stopped being there in my mind. I jerked back to reality when I felt a sharp, prickling pain on my leg. The smell of cigarette smoke came to me next, and I heard myself whimper and then scream when the prickling grew to a burning sensation. And then it stopped, and my scream became a whimper again. He did it one more time before I was allowed to remove myself once again, temporarily, from my world.

After that, for many weeks, he became remorseful, in his own way. He brought me fruits and ointments, and he did not speak to me unless it was to ask, in a gruff voice, if I needed anything from the market. He did not look me in the eyes, not in those days of him struggling to be different. And I stayed away from him in bed, and did not speak to him except to say yes or no, imagining that I was punishing him. But when he started to shed his ill-fitting skin and be more like his old self again, and come home after I was asleep, and not bring me fruits anymore, I slid into that version of me that wanted to be wanted, the version I had become soon after I had entered this marital agreement. Or maybe I had always been like this.

So, when a month or two or three went by, I put on the blue sari and the gold jewelry. When my husband saw me he laughed, but not in a mean way, and said I reminded him of an actress he had seen in a movie recently. I began to tug off the bracelet but he pulled me onto his lap. "I can see movies with my friends, can't I?" he said. It was a question but there was a statement, a warning, beneath it, and it felt good to be held. So I said yes, yes he could. And I thought, *This is a good change.*

It was after he carved into my chest with a rock, because he thought I had insulted him, because I had asked him about his sales, because he had sold the jewelry, that I put away the sari. And I washed my hair less and less, and let it get rough from not being brushed for days on end. I got into a habit of ignoring him.

Sometimes I thought about asking some woman in the Town over for tea, but the idea of making conversation seemed exhausting. Nobody really stepped closer to me in streets; perhaps they were wary of approaching the wife of the well-to-do furniture man. Or maybe they knew about us and wanted to stay away, as if trouble were contagious.

He left me after some time—I am not sure if it was a few months or many—and called me once from the City to tell me that he didn't think he was coming back. He was not completely unkind; he assured me that I could go on staying in the house in the Town.

It took time getting used to being there all by myself. It was not a big place but the rooms felt very empty to me. I made sure to pray in a different one each day. I performed the motions with energy. I learned to economize in new ways the food I was able to buy with the money my husband sent me; it was never the same, nor given at scheduled intervals. Loneliness sharpened the few words I exchanged with shopkeepers; hunger hollowed my stomach but thickened my skin. I went to a woman for help and did not take it personally when she said no. When the Town's water supply became strictly rationed, I began to go to the river to get my own.

Sometimes I saw a boy there. He came with a friend or two. Their conversations amused me. I thought I could tell them apart by their voices but I couldn't be sure. Having them there made me feel as if I had friends, especially the boy whose was Baadal.

I knew there were people who had decided to live for a while by the river. I never considered becoming one of them, not even when I felt disappointed when Baadal wasn't there, keeping me company unknowingly. One such time, I was walking away, a little sad and tired, and a woman approached me and said, not unkindly, "I could give you a sheet if you like, you could stay next to me under that tree over there." I said thank you but I had to go. She moved in a step closer and put a hand on my arm. "We all need to do our part." I pushed her hand away and went home.

2

LATER LESSONS

I HEARD BAADAL SAY, "I love you, I want to marry you," and I thought, *This is my weakness.* And "this" was many things: a solid roof, some-body who looked at me as if they wanted me even though I could see it ending so-and-so days or years later through disease or death or a ceasing of longing. The word *love* was a weakness—to hear that word. I had said it to Baadal the night he hurt that man because I felt the need to say it more than I felt the meaning of it. After he left, holding half of the biscuit I had put in his mouth, I went to the place he had mentioned. I found the man on the ground. His face was resting against an arm. No sound came from him, but maybe he was only asleep. I crouched next to him, picked up a rock, and brought it down on his head. On my way back to my little home, a cool night breeze pushed me from behind.

I said to Baadal, "Yes, I will marry you." After that he squeezed my hand and said we will go to an imam in the morning.

"What time?" I asked, as if we were deciding when to go buy eggs. He said, "Ten all right?"

He stayed until the sun started to go down. After he left I started tidying up what little I had to put away. I closed the sun-lightened cardboard about me and drew the cloth roof over my head. I slept early, and well. An hour after dawn, I was ready. I had folded every-thing and knotted the mouths of my plastic bags and zipped shut the other bag. I combed my hair and tied it with a ribbon. A little before ten I carried everything to the park entrance. Baadal arrived on a motorbike in his school shirt and pants. He looked as if he had got a haircut, and he smelled of cologne. I didn't ask him, but he told me that the bike was Nasir the barber's; Baadal had paid him the rental out of his savings. We hung most of my things from the handlebars but two of the items I had to carry on my lap, an arm around them. I put my other arm around Baadal's waist for balance. Closeness to him felt slightly unreal, but it wasn't because I had imagined this moment. More like I had transcended into a future I could not have predicted. Before we left, he asked if I was feeling okay, and I nod-ded, and couldn't help but smile.

We went to an imam in a mosque on the other side of Town, beyond which were narrower highways leading to villages. The pa-pers signed and the dua recited, Baadal and I exited the courtyard as husband and wife to no ceremony. He managed to work the straps of all of my bags around the handlebars this time. Now I put both my arms about him. He told me he was taking me to the City as a surprise celebration trip before we went to his home. I thought about that word; a different bed for me to sleep on, a door to close securely upon the night.

A little into the City Baadal seemed to have lost his way. He went twice around a roundabout, getting off on a road that took us farther away from where we wanted to go to. I could feel his shirt dampen-ing. Without warning, he turned the bike around, right on that main road, and now we were clinging to the side, going in the opposite direction against heavy traffic.

"This looks like a one-way road," I said, as trucks and buses rushed past us, dangerously close.

"I know what it looks like." His words were clipped.

His muscles relaxed when we reached shops and walking streets, and, consequently, my fingers loosened their clutch on his shirt a little. By an ice cream kiosk, he bought us vanilla cones, smiling again and looking like a schoolboy. A child came over to our bike, holding roses and jasmines. Baadal asked for a bracelet of jasmines, which was cheaper, then very carefully put it around my wrist. He said he wanted to take me to the seaside but was worried there wasn't enough petrol in the tank. I said we had a lifetime to go to the seaside.

The moment those words came out, I became filled with nervousness about his mother. I would call her Raheela aunty. Quickly, before we set off, I asked for the child to come back. I asked Baadal to get a rose and a jasmine bracelet for his mother; these would be gifts from me. He said, kindly, "Koka's mother accepted his wife just one week after he brought her home. My mother will like you, don't worry. Besides, it's my home too."

3

OBJECTS

I

I HAD LIVED BY MYSELF for such a long time, I had gotten out of the habit of worrying about dust on objects, or about the age of the sheet on my bed, or how rough my hair felt between the tips of my fingers, or about the crookedness of my teeth. The sheet I had been sleeping on for the last two months or so was a faded light blue with horizontal white stripes that thinned and thickened up and down the length of the fabric. I used to lie on it in a way that made the stripes go alongside my body, arranging myself so that I covered no more than six lines. Every two weeks, I slept on the next six lines until I ran out of clean sheet, after which I gave it a quick soak in a little water from the river. Now, with another person living with me, I would have to wash more often, myself and the sheet and everything else.

When Baadal and I spent our first few days as husband and wife in the park by the river, I found the old cardboard boundary too small to contain both of us and was unable to find another. So on the sixth day I expanded our walls by bringing over wet earth in fistfuls and making a new, low section. But twice Baadal accidentally made part of the paper wall come down when trying to climb over it instead of crawling through the panel that I had turned into a door. Then a strong, dry wind came from across the river and made the structure judder all afternoon and evening. Baadal wasn't there; he had left in the morning. I was by myself, trying to hold it all up. In the evening, when he came back with a paper bag of chana daal from Khushi's house, I was waiting for him, sitting on the folded cardboard, sheets and other belongings packed up.

We found shelter in Chacha Ameer's house for a few nights. We got to sleep on a good bed. There, for the first time under an electric light, I waited patiently while Baadal saw the cigarette burns on the backs of my thighs and the long, elegant cut on my chest created from the tip of a sharp piece of rock, all having settled into scars for some time now. All signs of my previous husband, I had been sure to tell him, just in case he thought it was the man I had first married. The marks distressed Baadal. He sat on the bed in tears, not knowing which way to turn me, and I burst out laughing and told him to keep his eyes closed or turn off the lights. He did both, and learned fast to snatch away his fingers if they happened upon a scar.

In just under a week, though, we had to leave that bed and that light. Baadal discreetly moved us to a corner of the small courtyard in his friend Juman's house. Sometimes, Juman's mother came out of her room and asked us how her son was. We lied and said he was getting healthy by the river. At night, we lay down on the old doubled blanket, not touching each other, too aware of the sky over our eyes and the pain in our stomachs. Always, at some point, Baadal fell asleep, but I stayed awake longer and longer.

And then, food began to arrive. Every few days, Raheela aunty came to the gate of the house and handed over one or two small, oily bags to Juman's mother. I started sleeping again. My shrinking stomach had started causing certain thoughts to balloon in my head; the image of Juman's father raging back into the house in the dead of the night and setting everyone on fire, for instance. With some food inside me now, my mind became rational once again. "You'll tell us if you hear from your husband, of course?" I asked Juman's mother. Our host clicked her tongue and said of course. I was even able to hold up a slice of buttered bread and think, *I am eating something carried in the hands of a woman who spit on me.* I shrugged and licked the butter. Juman's mother watched me, and then did the same.

The food was unusual, rich with oil and full of flavors I could not identify. "Where is your mother getting this from?" I asked Baadal. I was feeling stronger and more emboldened to ask difficult questions. Baadal, who only watched me consume the offerings and never touched any of them himself, opened his mouth then closed it, and gave his head a little shake. "It's from that man Junaid's house. I heard she helps him with chores."

A few more days of nourishment enabled me to convince Baadal to ask his father for Nabeela khaala's address in the City.

"I'm not going to go to her like a beggar," Baadal said.

"How can you ever be a beggar?" I replied, keeping my tone robust as if dispelling a child's illogical worry. "You have a *house* here, you're just not living in it. Pfff. You are the opposite of a beggar. And you are looking for a job, right? In the City!"

It was true; Baadal was spending hours and hours looking for employment far away.

This made me feel hopeful and happy. And his absence gave me the physical space to move around without bumping into him.

Juman's father returned late one night, without warning, and we were woken by the sound of a rock being thrown through a window. I knew right away who it was. Staying in a crouch, I stuffed the sheet into a bag, grabbed Baadal's hand, and ran for the gate. Once the house was out of sight we stopped and caught our breaths.

"He's going to kill her," I said.

Baadal looked at his feet. "I forgot my shoes there."

"Do you want to put on mine? We could take turns."

Baadal said, "Let's keep going."

We walked all the way to Chacha Ameer's shop. It was dark inside and the door was locked so we sat outside it to rest for a while. Baadal fell asleep, stretched out on the step, his head on a bag. When he woke up, we went on. Several minutes later, we found a pair of shoes. They looked like the kind someone would wear to an office; they did not have any laces. Baadal tapped the dust off them smartly, put his feet inside, and pronounced the shoes comfortable.

When we arrived at what looked like the edge of the Town, we were only a little surprised. I said, "We might as well go on into the City. There's nothing back there." This buoyed us. The brightening of the sky reduced our tiredness. We marveled at each other's endurance and how far we had walked. I asked Baadal to repeat his aunt's address out loud so I could memorize it, and he made a little song out of it, which was silly and made us laugh.

II

Every evening, in our shack under a bridge with the tin roof over our heads, Baadal and I spread open that day's newspaper that he brought back from his work at the electric company. I could not read much but I looked hard at any photographs of neighborhoods in the City. Baadal read out crime reports and we discussed which areas we should go see. On Sundays we went out with the list in hand. We became better at estimating distances between places. Then Baadal told me that someone at work could take us to see an apartment which might be within our budget. The man's name was Muneer. He picked us up in his car from a roundabout on a nearby main road. He did not know we lived under a bridge; Baadal hadn't wanted to tell him. Keeping parts of our truth to ourselves did not matter anyway because we treated ourselves and our home well. I had made the shack a comfortable and clean place for us, and my husband could leave for work every morning looking polished and professional.

As Muneer drove, he talked about the wonderful deal he'd got for the car; his sister's husband had known the seller. "If you ever need a car, you come straight to me," Muneer said. Baadal asked him where the apartment was and Muneer said a name which I could not remember from the newspapers. Forty minutes later, Muneer announced, "Almost there now."

"This is a decent neighborhood," Baadal said.

"This is a big city. There are plenty of decent neighborhoods for all kinds of people."

The apartment he showed us, and which we ultimately took, was on the twelfth floor. It had a bedroom, a living room, a kitchen, and a bathroom. It was very small, but I was struck with joy at the strong, good smell of detergent everywhere. I liked the clear glass on the windows in the living room through which I could see a busy road in the distance and a patch of green with a seesaw right below.

My favorite approach to our new home was by the broad main road. On one side of it were wide-trunked trees that looked like trustworthy guards of the fortress-like concrete walls behind them. All the way across the four lanes of that road, divided by an island, was a more accessible area: a line of shops crammed with TVs and water coolers, footpaths covered with people, and garbage containers filled with plastic bags and peels and rinds. I had to go behind this section of commerce to a block of apartments. On that street, different types of children ran on the broken sidewalks. They wore jeans with the cuffs folded high. A lot of these children's eyes were outlined thickly with kohl. The apartment blocks were in clusters, each one with its own pair of gates large enough to let in a water tanker. Through one of those gates, rusting in places like most others, I walked past pillars still adorned with the fading posters of political rallies and religious gatherings, a line of parked motorcycles and small cars, and, finally, to the third building on the left, where we lived. In the afternoons and evenings, there were children running and playing. Their loud, confident voices bounced off walls and balconies overlooking the area below, their mothers shouting instructions or warnings down to them. I never dreamed about or desired having children, but I found great enjoyment in looking over my own balcony.

We were very careful how we spent the money Baadal earned at the electric company. We kept a little aside for him to give to his mother and father—I convinced him to do this. It wasn't an emotional decision but a technical one; I wanted to do the right thing. We set aside some amount as savings, and the leftover money was what we spent on food. We decided we were going to be very strict and prudent. Baadal waited half a month before buying a pedestal fan and a wall clock. He also gave a little extra cash to a man from the telephone company to hurry up getting our line in order. He took me grocery shopping and we came home with a chicken and some vegetables. I tried to cook a dish we had eaten at his aunt's house, but it turned out too watery. Baadal said that when we got a TV I could watch some programs about cooking. I told him we ought to be more prudent on spending, though I also thought it would be lovely to have a TV and was so curious about what came on it. I had never had one.

I reveled in new ways of being busy. I hammered a nail in the living room wall and hung the shiny clock on it. I climbed up a stepladder and unscrewed the rods in the bedroom and put in place a pair of new curtains made of thin brown material I had bought for very cheap. I hung the same type of curtains in the living room. The sun did not appear in that window but in the evening, when it went down, I thought the combination of brown curtain and pinkish-orange sky was very pretty. One evening, I saw a pair of eggs on the windowsill. Carefully, I swung open the pane; there was no nest. For the next few days, I saw a bird land next to the eggs, then fly away. I held my breath as the small, smooth objects—I imagined them to be smooth and cool in the palm of my hand—rolled about a little. On the sixth day, I resolved to stick a shallow bowl on the windowsill, fill it with twigs, and put the eggs inside. When I took my nest to the window, I found the eggs gone. The area was just a little over the length of my arm but still I checked along it repeatedly, frantically. The eggs had fallen over the edge. Later, I paused in my dusting to see the bird arrive at one of its usual times. She—for I thought it was the mother bird—walked to both ends and pecked the concrete. She did this for a few more days before she stopped visiting. I was sad about this, and when I told Baadal, he was sad too. For a minute, we sat on the sofa, holding hands, looking at the window. I said to him, "I don't particularly want to be a mother, I probably won't be good at it."

He said, "You wanted to save those eggs. That was a kind thing to do. All a parent needs is to be kind, really."

Those early weeks in our new lives were good. Baadal liked the steadiness of our routine. It was disturbed only once, when his mother called to tell him she was planning to marry Junaid. He hung up the phone with force and refused to speak the rest of the day.

Over the days, I became better at finishing my work early. There was no water to carry from a faraway place, so I had time on my hands. I started to rest in the afternoons. I lay down on the bed, the air from the fan cooling my face. The light coming through the curtains was the color of cough syrup. Once, I was woken up from the ringing of the phone. I said hello but there was no answer from the other end, only the sound of breathing. "Raheela aunty, if this is you, then Baadal is at work at the moment," I said, "but I will tell him to call you as soon as he is back." I spoke slowly and avoided saying the word home. I held my breath, then heard a click and the dial tone. When Baadal came home, I did not tell him about the call.

He bought a TV, a small color one, that a man at an electronics shop sold to him for reduced installments. After Baadal put the big box down on the table, he brought up someone from the market below to help him fix the antenna, "like a brother would help a brother," he kept saying to the man. The TV was set up on a corner of our table in the living room. I learned the order of programs. Breakfast talk, religious lessons, poultry farming, thirty minutes of a drama, news at noon, lessons from an open university, then an hour's break during which a circle showed continuously. It was filled with a rainbow of bars, as well as black, white and gray lines, and squares. Then at four in the afternoon, the transmission flickered back to life with a children's show, a short cartoon in a language I didn't understand, a cooking show, evening news, a more exciting late-evening show with film stars and music stars and jokes full of innuendoes, thirty minutes of a new episode of a drama (I watched them all but had my favorites), the news at nine, a national song, and, at the very end, words of advice about life by a man and a woman.

Baadal got all of Sunday off from work. That was the day he and I usually went out exploring. By our second month in the apartment, we had been to the country founder's mausoleum, the sea, two popular shopping areas, an art gallery which had free weekend admission, and an expensive neighborhood. Some Sundays we went to visit Nabeela khaala.

There were a lot of rooms in her house, and a lot of people living in them. The aunt herself, her sons, and the wife and children of one of them. The first time Baadal and I had gone to see his aunt, the two women surrounded me. They had taken my handbag from me and swept me into a living room and said they could not believe Baadal had gotten married and brought over his bride so unceremoniously. Later, Asma, the wife of the older son called Karim, took me up a flight of stairs, showing me the spare bedroom with its attached bathroom, and asked wouldn't I please stay overnight? She held my hand and pulled me in and out of the rest of the bedrooms, then back downstairs into the kitchen with the off-white tiles halfway up the wall behind the four-burner stove, and then into all the areas where people could sit (drawing room, living room). No part of any room was dusty.

When it was just me and Baadal, whether in the Town or the City, I felt as if time were slow, like thick warm clay. When we went to his aunt's house, time seemed to move faster. We seemed to never return to our little home before dark. And during our whole day at his aunt's, I did not see Baadal much. His cousin Karim liked to sit with him with a pen in his hand and the Want Ads section of the newspaper spread out before them. I wished Baadal would say he wasn't looking for a different job, but he didn't, just listened and nodded and made notes. While he was busy this way, Asma stayed by my side. She said we ought to go shopping and pay a visit to a salon. She put her three children—a three-year-old boy, a two-year-old girl, a one-year-old girl—on my lap. Once, during a moment when Nabeela khaala was attending a phone call and Asma was busy with a child, I tried to silently wash dishes in the kitchen. But the women discovered me and led me away with soft scoldings.

They gave me their old clothes which I did not mind, because they felt the right kind of soft on my body, not the worn-out kind. They talked to me about themselves. The aunt said to me, "I have never liked Baadal's name. I wish he would change it to something more regular. Here in the City people with odd names stick out like misfits; they tend to clump up together like wet sand. I think if he changed his name, he would get a better job much faster. You have such a nice, normal name."

Another time, I was told by Asma, in a flood of words, the story of how she got married. "I wanted to get settled, be in my own home," she said. But it wasn't right to show her eagerness, so when her mother started talking about husbands, Asma made half-hearted protests. Her mother had found a matchmaker, a woman called Parveen. Parveen aunty liked to sit sideways at their table, her cotton qameez stretched out between her wide-apart knees. Two of her front teeth were stained and there was a small gap between them. She always wore a gold bangle, making sure it stayed below the cuff of her full, black sleeve. Asma wished the woman would leave before her other sisters came home from school, but the matchmaker liked to linger. Her mother would say, "Say salaam to Aunty, girls," and Aunty would smile and say, "Don't call me that, anybody can be an aunty. I am your khaala." Then she would turn to their mother. "Am I not like your big sister?" Asma understood the necessity of tolerating her.

One afternoon, Parveen aunty collected them in a rickshaw and took them to see a potential husband. "I was pressed against that woman," Asma said. "My mother's thigh was bony and I never minded being next to it, but Parveen aunty's thigh was soft." Asma shuddered, then laughed. "Would you believe, I thought he was a tailor. I don't know how that idea got into my head. I thought, all day long he measures women. How does he hold his inch-tape when he wraps it around their bust or stretches it down their arm?" Asma said the living room was nice, and aunty seemed nice. And then this young man entered. He had a moustache and a beard, not the big kind. "I thought he was all right. And he wasn't a tailor, of course. He was doing something much better than that."

"Tell us about yourself, Meena," they asked suddenly one afternoon. And, carefully, I talked about my house in the Town but not the husband I had lived with in it; about our decision to come to the City and not Raheela aunty's words; about finding our perfect apartment but not the bridge that had come before it. There were stories they could accept and those they could not. In this way, I stayed within their familial circle. I kept being invited to sit at their table, shell peas and pick stones out of rice, and eat hot food with them.

Baadal was usually quiet when we returned from these visits, but I did not think anything of it. But one night, when I showed him a shirt Asma had given to me, he shook his head. "You've got to stop this poor person's habit of taking people's used belongings." And though his words were unkind, I understood why he said them. When he said one weekend that he did not feel like visiting anyone, he was tired, that was all right too.

It had been a while since he and I had gone out together to discover a new place or to revisit an old one. I didn't burden him with requests, it wasn't my way. I began walking different routes when doing errands. The main road bored me now; I had seen all the cars that came out from behind the high walls, the women in the backseats and the drivers in the front. I explored the opposite side. There, girls walked in groups and boys smoked on street corners. Some went by slowly on their motorbikes. Sometimes a girl would be standing very close to a boy, sharing a cigarette with him, and sometimes she would be on the back of a bike. I began to describe these scenes to Baadal, but when he rubbed his eyes I knew he was only pretending to listen.

One day, on the way home, I bought a pair of birds from a woman who sat behind a row of noisy wire cages on the footpath. I held the small wire dome between my hands. The birds were small, one blue and the other yellow-green. "Aus-tray-liyan parr-it," the woman had said. I repeated it to Baadal when he came home. He looked at the birds for a moment then corrected me, "Australian parrot." His r still rolled but there was none of the seller's hesitation.

"What are they going to eat?" he asked, frowning slightly.

"Nothing special," I said.

I gave them tiny pieces of vegetables from my plate, even meat, whenever we had it. At first, I did this without thinking in front of Baadal, but when once or twice he sighed and shook his head, and I learned that it was not in indulgence, I fed the birds before he came home, keeping them caged in the kitchen. At night before going to sleep I covered their cage with an old ragged cloth to keep them quiet. In the day I let them shriek as loud as they wanted to. Once, I let them fly free in the bedroom, tricking them back inside the cage later with birdseed. But they had left droppings on the curtains and the bedhead, and I spent a long time scrubbing them away and checking for marks.

It wasn't that Baadal was an angry man. It was just that one day he asked me why the windows were looking so grimy. He went over to each of them and dragged his fingers down first the inside then the outside of the panes. He held up gray fingers a few inches away from my eyes. "The windows at my house were this color," he said. "They can't be this color here. There's no *need* for them to be this color here." Then he grabbed a rag from somewhere in the kitchen and spent the next half an hour wiping all the windows clean.

It seemed to irritate him that I didn't have friends.

"I don't need them," I said.

"That is not natural. You don't think it's unnatural?"

"No."

"But—but they could tell you about hair and clothes, things like that."

"What's wrong with my clothes?"

He waved a hand. "Well, that shirt you're wearing. You sewed it yourself, right? A woman friend could tell you where you could find a good tailor so you wouldn't have to go on looking like the old way."

I thought Baadal was being silly talking about women's clothes. It was interesting, though, to imagine conversations with a neighbor.

"That woman on our floor always smiles at me with all her teeth whenever we see each other," I said, half thinking out loud. "She would ask how we got married."

"Make something up."

"I will tell her Asma's story."

"Good. Good. We live in the City now. We need to completely belong here."

A few weeks later, Baadal brought over a man to paint the kitchen because he said the yellow was too dark, too sad. We didn't have the money for it, and I wondered who he had borrowed from. But still I decided that these were the nicest days in my life. Never before had I lived in blocks of worry-free time which were longer than a half hour or half a day. Two whole days could go by with my mind occupied by the pleasant fog of dusting, cooking, resting. I was surprised at how I had become used to water coming out from any tap at any time, even if sometimes it was just a trickle. I became very good at purchasing, in one morning, cushions, combs, slippers, and a one-kilogram bag of rice, to keep the appearance of fullness in our small space. Each time I bought something it made Baadal happy, and that made the distance between the edge of the City and the Town seem to grow longer. Our small apartment became crowded with reminders of our improved lives: the plastic cover for our table, the six-sided mirror on the wall, the two types of daal and the big bottle of ketchup, the wooden sign that I hung over our bedroom door which the shopkeeper assured me read WELCOME TO

Our Happy Home. In the bathroom, mint toothpaste instead of the tooth powder.

∽

On a morning in August, Baadal and I woke up to rain. We went to the window in the living room that gave us a bigger view of the sky and, in silence, watched wet cars and trucks and buses drive over the shining gray road.

"You don't have an umbrella," I said after a while.

"I'll run to the bus."

The rain made me feel new and clean. The clothes that got wet in the little balcony did not bother me, and, later, the smarting of my eyes and the tears that flowed out of them as I cut onions in the kitchen did not bother me. Even when the electricity went out at three in the afternoon and the rooms became dark and stuffy, I was all right. I opened the balcony door and the window to let in some rain-darkened light. Even when Baadal came home a lot later than usual, at least an hour, tired, irritable, and soaked. Three nights in a row, we ate dinner in the dark and went to bed in our warm room, the window and balcony door shut to keep out air and burglars. Baadal was too tired to talk, and there was nothing new I had to say about my day. I spread my hair behind me on the pillow and lay quietly. A few children still played in the rain in the courtyard. Slack mothers, I thought mildly. A generator somewhere was going to start soon, drowning all other sounds. I felt a thrill when the roar of its electric power ripped through the air. Enveloped in its loudness, I looked at the fan hanging from my ceiling, willing it to turn on.

One night, my face and body damp with sweat, I crept to the living room and softly opened the window, keeping a hand on the latch. I heard a noise behind me and turned swiftly, pulling the window shut. Baadal shuffled in and sat heavily on the sofa, arms over his knees and head hanging low. "I'm going to buy a generator," he said, his voice raspy with sleep. But he couldn't, of course, I knew; it was more than we could afford. At a break in the rain the following day, I went out and bought him an umbrella.

III

I was coming back from the vegetable market when the woman who lived next to me entered the compound with me. I had heard someone—a cousin or a sister or a friend—call her Sajida. We said salaam to each other and got into the four-person lift with our bags. The metal box moved slowly, creakingly, and Sajida gave me a companionable, nervous smile, which I returned. Her white face powder did not reach her hairline, showing a thin line of skin. At the fourth floor, the lift stopped, but nobody pulled the door open from the other side to come in. I clicked my tongue and Sajida shook her head, both of us probably imagining naughty children who rang doorbells and called lifts then ran away. The box started to move again with a groan, and then stopped.

"Why has the lift stopped?" Sajida asked.

"Maybe the electricity has gone out." I was trying to sound calm only because her smile had disappeared.

"But it's not three o'clock. And that light up there is on."

I pushed the number 12 button on the panel, but nothing happened. I pushed at the door to open it but it did not move. "Somebody open the door!" Sajida bellowed from behind me. I knocked on the metal, first with the joint of my finger then with my knuckle. "*Baji*, wait," a boy said from the other side. More voices joined him, and hands began to tug at the handle. The door popped open and I stepped out, my foot landing awkwardly because the lift was about two inches above the floor. Sajida followed in the same manner.

The gaggle of boys parted when one of them said, "Give them space." I recognized his voice as the one who had first spoken to us from outside the lift. He was already moving on. Quickly, I pulled out a note out of my purse and held it out to the boy. He blushed, took the money, mumbled, "Thank you, Aunty," and fled to the stairs.

Sajida and I continued our long journey upward, on foot now, sometimes pausing, Sajida more often; my legs still remembered a little of that very long walk I had done with Baadal. When we reached our floor, I said to Sajida, "Why don't you come in for a cup of tea?"

The TV had already taught me many useful things, such as special prayers to recite; a kind-looking man with a close white beard and thick black-framed glasses said them out loud slowly, and I repeated them in my sitting room. I asked God for material success and afterlife success; for health; for getting rid of anxiety; for the words with which to talk to Him about how sharp and right the rock had felt in my hand the night I felt compelled to protect Baadal. I had bought myself a second prayer rug and a rosary. Sajida, on her afternoon visits, brought other kinds of useful knowledge. She told me to look out for the little rectangle of scholarly instruction that appeared on the top of page three in the Sunday newspaper.

"What kind of instructions are they?"

"Oh, anything. Personal beauty, kitchen hygiene, marriage advice for women. You should cut them out and save them. It's wrong to throw away wise words. They just end up with fishmongers who wrap up smelly fish heads with them."

"I cannot read very well."

"Doesn't matter. Keep them in a drawer in the kitchen anyway. Your life will improve."

Baadal came upon those cutouts one day when he was looking for a pen. He sifted them through his fingers and said, "Is this a new hobby? Can you tell what they say?"

I shrugged. "No, but some have words that look like those on TV with the maulana."

Baadal picked one up and held it closer to his face. "Remember your mistakes. Ask Allah for forgiveness. Remember your blessings. Thank Allah for them."

"They're just something Sajida told me about."

"Is that your new friend?"

"I think so."

"Well, that's a good development, that's an improvement over those birds." He put back the little rectangle of paper and shut the drawer. He took out a slice of bread. He looked around as if searching for something. He leaned against the doorframe, put a hand into a pocket, and bit into the plain bread. "I do that, you know."

"Do what?"

"Remember my mistakes and ask for forgiveness."

Did Baadal put his forehead on the ground and say sorry to Allah over his mistaken belief that he had severely hurt that man? I had never told him what I had done that night. I couldn't let Baadal know how much I had let myself need him.

I got up and took the bread from his hand. "I will make you a proper sandwich."

In the house I used to live in with my mother, we had shared a room. I slept on the same bed as her. I liked to lie at the foot of it so that my mother and I were like a triangle without a base. She had a corner in that room where she kept a short pile of books. Three, probably. They were books of prayers and explanations of those prayers.

My mother could not read much but every night she opened the books one by one and practiced a page out of each, putting her finger under each word that she said out loud. Then she copied the sentences into a notebook. The exercise took her almost until midnight. Sometimes I would ask her what was in her book. She would wait until the end of a word before saying, in her voice which had become a little raspy, that it was a short prayer about health, or happiness, or both, and she would point out a word for me to see. Most of the time, though, I was content to quietly play with my doll, and if bored with that, then with my imagination, falling asleep while she studied.

As I clipped my prayers from the newspaper, I wondered how many new formations of words from familiar letters my mother had learned to make.

It was toward the end of that year, when the temperature in the air had dropped and I was wearing my first sweater in the City, that we got a call from Baadal's mother with the news that his father was very ill. As Baadal got ready to leave, I wanted to ask him how long he thought he would be gone; the life we had constructed seemed suddenly unpredictable, breakable. What I said instead of that was, "Tell your father I am praying for him to get better. Bring him back with you if you can." While Baadal was gone, I fed my birds and assured Nabeela khaala over the phone that I was perfectly alright on my own. By the first night, Baadal had not come back. I could not sleep from misery. I thought, *I will lose everything.* I put the bird cage next to me on the sofa and watched TV until late. When the stations shut down, I took the birds to the bedroom and slept, my body's basic need taking over.

Baadal returned on the afternoon of the second day, and I was relieved, especially when he told me about something he had seen that had made him laugh. I thought, *Life has gone back to normal.* He left every Friday to see his father with a change of clothes and a little money. I got used to that. He did not always remember what he was saying, and his clothes hung loosely on him, and the wad of notes he stuffed into his wallet to take to the Town became thicker and thicker, and that was all right because he had a father and a mother who needed all of that—him and the cash and other invisible ways he was expending himself, out of duty and guilt—and I knew those were feelings I could not understand, because I did not think in terms of *father* and *mother*, and still all that was all right, it was bearable, as long as he returned on the last bus on Sunday and went to work Monday through Friday and ate dinner with me at night while a drama played on the television.

I waited for Baadal's father to get better, but in the winter of that year, he needed some tests done at the hospital in the Town. Baadal used the advance on his salary. We could not pay our phone and electricity bills. He told me he was going to borrow from Karim, and before I could say anything, he went on, a little belligerently, that Karim was family and we did not have any alternative. So on a Saturday, Baadal first went to his aunt's house, and then to the bank. He did not speak much to me at home afterward. His sulkiness continued until one evening when he pointed to the TV and said, "I am going to get a bigger one."

I tried to choose my words carefully. "Maybe we should wait a little."

He said, "I know someone who knows a man who sells electronics at less than the market price."

The promise of a new item for our small home in the City made him change from a moody sadness to a moody happiness. He wanted me to come with him. It turned out that the man at the electronics shop did not have any TVs in our price range, so Baadal bought a toaster instead. On the way to the bus stop, brand-new cardboard box in his hands, he saw through the window of another shop plates, platters, sets of cutleries. "Those are like the ones at Nabeela khaala's house," he said. He went in and I followed. He insisted that I choose new plates. When I said we did not need to, he picked up a few heavy, delicate ones and pushed them into the shopkeeper's hand. At home, Baadal wanted to throw away our old steel plates.

"It doesn't make sense to waste them," I said evenly.

"Fine. Keep them, but I'm not going to use them." He hummed as he took out the new toaster and set it up in the kitchen. He told me to invite Nabeela khaala and her daughter-in-law over for tea. "In fact, tell them to come tomorrow morning, why wait."

So I called them, and poured tea into the new teacups and toasted bread in the shiny black machine and served cake and biscuits on the new plates. I left everything the way it was, clearing up only after Baadal had come home and glanced at all our new things.

But his irritability returned one night when, during an ad break, he said, "Why can't we have some meat?" and I said, "It has become expensive for us again." He pushed away his new plate, the corners of his mouth turning down like a child's. I sat next to him and fed him with my hands. On the TV, a camera moved across a room with sunshine-drenched off-white walls and gray granite counters. "American-style kitchen and open-plan living room," a woman's voice said, smoothly and with understated triumph. The room being shown had white semi-transparent curtains fluttering gently at a pair of open windows, on either side of which was a soft-looking single sofa. "At easy monthly installments."

Baadal put his arm around me and said, "We should move there." I leaned forward and changed to the other channel.

IV

At the start of the next year, Baadal convinced our landlord to take an advance on the total rent we owed him, promising that he would make the full payment before two months were over. He also bought a motorbike.

"Who gave you the money for that?" I asked him.

A friend, he said.

"Which friend?"

"The one who showed us the apartment."

We stood on opposite sides of our big table covered with the plastic. A small section of it had burned away when I accidentally set the iron on it. I said he had to think like an adult, not like an emotional sixteen-year-old, we got around just fine on the bus, the bike was a waste of money. He said if I went out and did some work, I would soon see what catching a bus in work clothes was really like.

"I have worked hard before and I can do it again." My voice shook with anger, rising with each word. "I will find better work than you, and I will take care of both of us, and your father and your mother and your whole damn family."

"And what about all these birds?" he said, shouting as well. "What about the ridiculous amount of money spent on them?"

"I feed them from my plate, they don't take anything from you. I would not dream of taking even a crumb from you."

"Every day it is: my birds did this, my birds did that. I am sick of hearing about them." Flecks of spit flew from his mouth.

"You have to decide where you want to be. Here, or back at someone's lawn in the Town with a drunk man running around!"

"Those birds are eating all my food!"

For three days after that I cooed and sang to my parrots and fed them pieces of bread from my own plate in front of Baadal. I knew he wasn't using the bike, not even to go to work, because he didn't take the key when he left in the morning. On the fourth day, I saw his angry, miserable face, and relented. I said to him, "We might as well use the bike now that it's here." So we rode on it all the way to Nabeela khaala's house to show it to her.

❧

Before winter made way for spring, Baadal lost his job. There was a shuffling of departments at the electric company, he said, and suddenly his position did not exist anymore.

"But big companies always need clerks," I said, sitting down slowly.

"Well, they don't need me."

He sold the motorbike and took money from his aunt so we could stay another month in our apartment. He made her promise not to tell her sons, not even the one who had moved to another country. Baadal left in the morning to search for work, coming back at night. Sometimes he ate dinner, other times he went straight to bed. I could only leave him alone. We sold the TV. We let our phone get disconnected. When we spoke at all, it was about asking the other to turn the fan on or off or to shut the window before bed.

"Let's move to Nabeela khaala's house for a while," I said to him. "Save some money until you find work."

"And lose this place?"

"Your aunt is paying for it anyway."

Baadal sucked in his breath sharply. "You know, a man set himself on fire last week because he had four little children and they were all starving. But look around you, we're so far from that. We've got all these curtains and plates and shiny clocks and those *birds*." His tone was bitter with mock pleasantness, rising in volume. "Look, Baadal,

I don't have any friends but look, these birds talk to me! Look how they shred the meat!"

His words fell upon me like cold water. He was right; the life I had built around myself was ridiculous. I went into the bedroom and shut the door. In a plastic bag, I put my oldest clothes from when I used to live in the Town, and my comb. The talcum powder and the small bottle of perfume on the shelf were only proof now of my foolish mind. I left them in their places. I fetched the birdcage from the kitchen and said to Baadal, "I am leaving."

"To Khaala's house? At this time?"

"Not to her house, not to any of your people's houses."

The skin on Baadal's forehead bunched up. "Then where the hell are you going?"

"I don't know."

I took a step toward the door but Baadal took two strides and was in front of me. He grabbed the birdcage and twisted it out of my hand. I lunged to get it back but he held it above my head.

"Give me back my birds." The words came out in a whisper. I was afraid I was going to begin crying.

His hair curling from the heat, eyes wide, he said, "We are going to live *here. Together.*"

"I don't want to live with you."

"Maybe you've got other plans. Maybe you want to see your exhusband, the one with that extra house in the Town. Is that right? Do you want to go to him?"

"You're a murderer."

And with that lie I made him irreversibly fallible in his own eyes, and made myself the better of us two. His mouth distorted in aggrieved, desperate anger. "I am not a murderer!" he roared. He pulled open the window and fumbled with the little latch on the door of the cage, tilting it. The water and seeds inside tipped over. One of the birds hopped to the opening and flew out of the window. I screamed and grabbed Baadal's sleeve and pulled hard. His arm came down, more easily than I had expected, and the metal of the cage caught me on my face and lip.

My mother used to say to me, "You are a strong, strong child, Meena. You are iron. You are steel." My husband Talib used to say to me, lovingly, "I don't have to worry about you. You will always find a way." My other husband, the one who left, used to say, "You are unbreakable." I sat on the pavement outside the apartment block, leaning against the wall. In front of me was the bus stop. My bag was on my lap, the birdcage at my feet. In my hand I held a piece of paper with an address on it, given to me by Sajida. The woman who lived there hired seamstresses. Sajida had said unaccompanied women in the City could live in hostels. She had never been to one herself but she had seen a program about them once. After I rushed out of my home, Sajida had let me come into her apartment but didn't ask me to sit down. She brought water and put some money into my hand, which I had pressed back, murmuring thank you and no. On the paper with the woman's address. Sajida had left off her own phone number.

The memory of this moment, of how I had allowed myself to depend on a stranger for unconditional help, would pinch me until, some fifteen years later, Asma would read out loud a story from a newspaper about how the faulty pipes in a building in Copper Market had cost a man his job and put his family in distress. The pipe in their bathroom had burst and flooded their apartment. The man had suffered electrocution. His wife Sajida was quoted as being devastated.

BAADAL, 1997

1

PEOPLE'S COLONY

It takes me almost forty-five minutes to walk from my new home to the restaurant, where I deliver food during the day, and thirty minutes to walk in the other direction to the hotel where I work the nightshift as a receptionist. Where Meena and I sleep now, where we have moved all of our belongings, is in a place called People's Colony—a collection of shacks and mostly unpainted bricks cemented together in a valley. The colony appears suddenly, naked and brown, as one crests one of two slopes—the "restaurant side" or the "hotel side." The restaurant slope is cleaner, the hotel slope has thorny bushes and rusted car parts and broken furniture. As ugly as that side is, the prospect from there is cheerful: a street lined with businesses lit up until midnight. There are fewer lights in the colony itself. At night, older men stand around in little groups in their white undershirts at corners of narrow dirt paths, smoking and lazily scratching their arms and stomachs. I listen to the drawl of their words as I pass them, and there is no discontent to be heard even though their many barefoot children run in and out of narrow doorways guarded with a metal door or a curtain of cloth.

The day we left our apartment and came to this hole, our little room in a squat, four-story building, Meena had walked slowly from the door to the two-burner stove in the opposite corner. She tried the tap in the sink next to it. A dribble of water came out, then died.

"The landlord says it's an issue with the pipes. He guaranteed he will have them fixed in a week," I said to her. "And he says they never have any problems with water here. And even then, a tanker comes twice a week, just in case."

"Where is the bathroom?"

My face became warm. "The building shares a bathroom. It's on the ground floor. Very clean."

Slowly, she walked to a corner and set down her handbag.

There are four doors on every floor. Multitudes of people seem to be living behind each one. There is always noise in the morning, when I leave for the restaurant, and at sunrise when I come back from the hotel. I wade through waves of dishes clanging, couples arguing, children shrieking, onions frying—why are the children not in school, why are these women always loud, the men always loud, their old always reclining. Why don't these people shut their damn doors. The first few days, Meena waited for me to wake up for my shift at the hotel so she did not have to go to the bathroom alone that late at night. Then she trained herself to go earlier, and less frequently.

It was terribly hard at first to stay awake all night behind the reception counter at the hotel. Jaafar became my friend. He is the doorman there. He is full of helpful tips. He told me I should get an hour's nap in the day at my other job. He says hardly anyone ever needs the front desk person during the night so if I doze off every now and then it will not be a problem. He showed me a jar of pills and said they help him stay awake and I could take a few if I liked. So I did, careful to take only one with my dinner as he said I should, because more could be dangerous. He'd said in about a week's time

I should be trained to stay awake without their help, but it's been a month now and I buy my week's quota from him. He assures me he is giving me a brother's discount. I still manage to have savings. I keep them in a drawer, in a sock at the bottom of my clothes.

Once, on a weekend when Meena and I were still new in the City, my cousin Karim had taken all of us out to the seaside. My aunt sat in the front. His wife Asma, her children, and Meena and I were in the back. She and I gazed at places we had never seen before, roundabouts off which shot smooth roads into deep recesses of big, colonnaded homes. After an hour or more we reached the sea. It was gray, full of movement, and loud. Above us the sky was gray as well. Vapor surrounded our bodies and covered our skins, entered our nostrils. Karim bought us ice cream, and when one of his children dropped her cone and cried he bought her another one and I thought, *That is what I will do one day: My child will cry and I will buy her two more cones.* Meena left our little group and walked to a man selling roasted chickpeas. She untied a corner of her dupatta, took out a note, paid the man, and passed on to Karim's children a cone of chickpeas. Later, I told her not to store her money the way poor people did.

☙

Jaafar asks me why my parents named me Baadal.

"I mean, *cloud*?" He grins but he is not mocking, I can tell. "*Cloud*. What kind of cloud anyway? A cute little white one, or a big gray thundercloud?"

I shrug. "Just one that gives shade, I suppose."

"You could change your name if you don't like it."

"How?"

"Well it's a long route to that. You'll have to go to the ID card office, there will be a long line there, you'll probably have to come back the next day. It could take a whole week or more."

At the hotel, we are not allowed to smoke. To pass our silent moments, we turn our attention to the voice from the radio. Somebody else is awake at that hour, talking about the history of a particular national song.

"Or you could just tell us to call you something else," Jaafar says.

"I wouldn't know what name to choose."

"Well, isn't there a name you like? A normal name, like Mohsin, or Hassan."

"I know a Juman. He's a friend from school. His mother didn't name him like us."

Jaafar shakes his head. "No, that's still a name loaded with origin. Has to be a placeless name. An any-man name."

The radio is now playing an old recording of a song. A woman's thick voice rises and dips.

"Yusuf," I suggest.

Jaafar nods appreciatively.

"Hello, I am Yusuf," I try out. "Yusuf Baadal. Baadal Yusuf."

Jaafar grins again. "You're never getting rid of what your mama gave you."

A car slowly comes to a stop outside. Jaafar goes to greet them and bring in their suitcases. I rub my eyes and straighten my shirt. I try to see if these guests are the tipping kind.

One early morning, after I am done at the hotel, I walk up to my apartment, through the nauseating smells of dinners and through the sounds, seeping out from under the doors, of people who cannot keep their voices down, when I see Juman propped against the wall next to my door, fast asleep. My breath becomes short. I shake his shoulder. His eyes open and he jumps to his feet, his face breaking into a grin.

"Is my father all right?" I ask him, my tongue dry.

Juman's smile vanishes. He says, nodding hard with every word, "Yes, yes! Everyone at home is okay! Your mother and father are fine."

A door opens on the floor above and suddenly feet are running down the stairs. A moment later two children in school uniforms with bulky bags on their backs run past me and Juman, down the next flight of stairs.

My heartbeat becomes normal, but the tiredness, which had fled at the thought of death, now returns, multiplied. I do not feel like speaking, I just want to sleep. But Juman is a friend.

"Come inside," I say. "When did you get here? Why didn't you go in?" I turn toward the door, rest my forehead on it, and knock. "It's me."

From the other side, the two latches and the main lock are undone. Meena stands to one side. She looks tired. She speaks to Juman first. "You will have breakfast here." To me she says, almost defensively, "Your friend did not want to come in," and goes to the stove. Juman slowly lowers himself onto a chair while I sit heavily on the sofa. There is a slight shadow on his face but his clothes look tidy, his shoes are without holes.

Meticulously, he recounts the brief history of his arrival: he had reached my place late, around eleven. He had thought I would be home by then. Meena answered. (Here, he laughs, not unkindly. "She looked as if Death itself was at the door. Just like you did today." I imagine Meena's heart rising to her throat; she would have thought something had happened to my mother or father. I hope she thought of my mother; I had only thought of my father.) Juman reassured her he was only here to see me, it had been such a long time. He insisted he would wait outside, even refusing a pillow Meena brought him.

He grins at me again and I see the gaps in his teeth. "So I finally get to see you at your home in the City." His eyes move around and I see the unpainted sections of walls, the mustard-yellow light from the bulb, the kind of light that, when naked, is the color of lack.

"This is a temporary place," I say. "We're just waiting to move, actually." I smile brightly, as if to show that a home like this is a necessary part of my plan all along. "How did you know where I was?"

"I went to your khaala's house. Kawsar had her address. She told me you were here. Easy."

Meena sets down a tray and goes back. Between me and Juman there is toasted bread, a jar of jam, and two fried eggs. Juman reaches for the bread and the knife. In a low voice meant to invite confidence or confession he says, "Two jobs? Are things all right?"

"All temporary, my friend," I answer loudly.

Juman nods and puts a piece of his egg in his mouth. "I will not take much of your time," he says, chewing. "You must be tired after working all night."

I shrug. Meena brings us two cups of tea and retreats again.

"I've been thinking about becoming a teacher here, you know," Juman says, "in a private school. Think they'll take me?"

"That's the good thing about this City. The place is full of schools. Every bungalow is a school. Some principal somewhere would take you."

"I've already found a place to live, a room with five or six other men, all of them laborers. Nothing like your fancy apartment here." He laughs when he says fancy, and I laugh too, my second time so far, but there is constraint in our sounds, not the freefall of old friendship.

"A roof over the head," I add.

"I've got the interviews lined up, and things are looking good. I just need some money for a little while. And I thought I could come to you. To tell you the truth, I did not even hesitate. I will pay you back next month."

I know if I look away from him, or blink, or say anything at that moment, it would show how I feel. Because now I am irritated. I am angry. My head begins to pound dully. He is lying about the interviews but he doesn't know that. He also doesn't know that he would not return the money. He is pretending to both of us. And I don't have money. I owe my aunt and my cousins. I am losing the things I had bought. I am desperately close to being sucked back into the Town, into that old life, the barrenness of those streets, the stillness of expectations there. All I do, though, is nod slowly, my eyes flicking involuntarily to the gaps in Juman's mouth.

"How much?" I ask, despite myself.

"Only two or three thousand, that's all."

And now I am shaking my head, lips forming a shape of tragic helplessness. "I don't have that kind of money."

Juman points at the yolk stains and the breadcrumbs. "You look like you're eating well, my friend." He laughs again, shorter, more abrupt, more false than before.

"Just the blessings multiplied from an honest living."

"You won't even miss the money. You've got your aunt's money."

I get to my feet quickly and my leaden head spins for a moment. I feel crushed with the weight of my friend's delusions. I remember how he had asked Kawsar and me for food once. I remember that his father drank. There are no interviews. He is losing his teeth. "I don't have anything to spare at the moment. You should go back to the Town, see if Chacha Ameer can give you something."

Juman has stood up as well. His face is red, his eyes wet.

I hold a chair for support. "Your condition right now, that is what bad living would do to you. We all make our choices. I choose to pay my bills and get the hell out of debt, make a good life, eat some meat. Don't be like your father." I stare at him, willing him to argue with me or hit me. But he just leaves.

———

"I am going to open a beauty parlor," Meena says.

It is morning, a few days since Juman was here. I rub the itch of tiredness from my eyes.

"Why?" I ask.

"I gave Ghulam Ali's wife's a haircut while you were gone. I also gave her a facial and a pedicure. She said my work was good."

My wife, washing other women's faces and feet, touching their oily scalps.

I say to her, "But we don't really need the money."

She shrugs. "Maybe not now. Anyway, I don't like being idle."

"What do you mean, not now? We aren't hungry, we don't sleep out in the open, we don't wear rags."

She takes a step back, a very small step. It is a move that is barely noticeable but it makes me stop.

Making her own tone lighter she says, "You won't even notice it. I will work while you are away."

Maybe the beginning of my failing was the day I was born, the day I caused my mother great physical pain. Or when I stole money from Chacha Ameer. Or the night I beat that man until he stopped fighting back. The consequences of unforgivable actions don't care about the reasons, they just keep recurring in the form of well-deserved hurts.

Meena buys a mirror from a shop that sells used items, and a hair dryer and a set of brushes from a woman in the Colony. She cleans the brushes two times, soaking them in water foamy with detergent, rubbing the bristles with her fingers, rinsing them under the tap. On a scratched-up whiteboard she gets one of the children in the area to paint the words: MEENA BEAUTY PARLOR – MONDAY TILL THURSDAY – 11AM TILL 7PM. She pays the child two rupees. She nails the sign to our front door. She tells me she will give me back the money she borrowed to get her supplies. I tell her it is her money too and all she says is, "Do you want tea?"

❦

If my father's blood pressure rises again, it could be fatal. On Friday evenings, before I make my weekly visit to him, I stand in front of my reflection in the mirror and practice smiling. Stress and unhappiness from me could make him die, so each visit I bring him a pair of presents: a bunch of bananas and no tension about his son; apples and no concerns about his son's life; coconut water and the relief of believing that his son is doing well. There is not a lot else that I can get for him anyway.

My father does not know that I am now a driver and a reception-ist. Even if he were well, I wouldn't know how to tell him; we don't have the kind of relationship where a father puts a hand on his son's shoulder and says words of advice about life and finances. What we talk about is the City. He likes to hear about my life there. I describe the people I remember from the electric company—Murtaza the boy who brings chai and makes sure he gets a tip from everyone, even if it's a coin; Ashraf sahab the secretary who has to tap his desk three times before he files papers. When no one else comes to mind, I make up a few—Miss Anam who works in a cubicle on the first floor and eats a bar of chocolate for lunch every day, a man called Raza who owns three cars and keeps a lion cub at his farmhouse. I tell my father some truths about the City, that at dusk the lights in the streets and roads turn on, all at the same time. I complain about the potholes in the street where my apartment is. He still believes that is where I live. He was very proud when I told him I bought a motorbike, so I keep on creating stories about that too. He asks about Meena. I tell him, "She is so happy there. She has bought herself a pair of little birds, they are noisy but very cheerful." For a moment I hesitate. "She has started a small business. A beauty parlor. Very popular with the building ladies." That seems to make him happy. He wants me to tell her she is a very smart woman.

My father likes to share his own little pieces of news. The milkman's son ran off with a girl. Or Bibi Sakeena's eye treatment is going to cost so much that she has decided to let the blindness take over. I lie down next to him and let my eyelids shut as he speaks. Sometimes I sleep for so long I wake up the next day. Before I leave, I hold out an envelope. It has the week's money for both him and my mother but what I always say is, "For you, Baba." And he nods with his head that I put it on his bed—he does not like to take it from my hand—and says, "I will be sure to pass this on to your mother."

On the bus back I sometimes pinch myself to stay awake but sometimes I cannot help falling asleep. It is a mistake when this happens because then that night I stay awake, my eyes closed, my body tired, my mind recalling, repeating, revising parts of the day, the week. Before the sun rises Meena wakes up for fajr prayer. Sometimes I pretend I have woken up with her at that very minute to keep her from asking me questions full of concern. And sometimes I don't care because my mouth is full of a sourness and my head is full of irritation. I do wuzu silently and finish my prayer and get into bed again, my back to Meena, to chase sleep for whatever time I have left. When she goes to the bathroom, I break my rule and take a pill for my morning.

These, then, are my days and my nights—the delivery bike on the road, the long hours in the hotel with Jaafar and the radio, and the money from both to pay for the medicine to take to my father and to pay for the bus rides from one home to another. In January the winter becomes bleaker and colder; the wind goes through my cotton sweater and into my skin; the taste of exhaust fumes on my tongue goes from thick to sharp. My father develops a cough so I buy him a syrup. I start making a pack of cigarettes last a week. Before I enter a pharmacy I recite two short prayers ten times each, no more and no less, always in the same order. If I make a mistake I begin again; I cannot risk having the prices of medicine go up. I cannot risk anything changing. If I keep illness away from me, and if I don't make a slip in my routine, then one day I can put everything back in its right place.

One evening I come close to disturbing this balance; Meena asks if I would like her to go with me to the Town. I am lying down with my arm over my eyes for a few minutes' rest before I leave, my bag next to me. The thought of the two of us with each other for all those hours making careful, polite talk—her because she senses my growing tension, me because I want to show my gratitude to her—makes me feel suffocated. Slowly, I lower my arm and tell her a lie, that my father would be embarrassed to have his daughter-in-law see him in that tiny room. She does not ask again.

But one Wednesday morning I enter my home to find her standing, waiting for me. Your father is in the hospital, she says.

This time, she is with me on the bus. She has insisted upon coming. It doesn't matter anyway. I keep my face looking straight ahead while she leans hers against the window. She is next to me as we enter the old, diminished hospital and as we climb the stairs to the first floor.

Kawsar is standing in front of one of the beds, his back to us. My mother is sitting in a chair, listening to a man in a white coat. They turn when they hear me. She appears the same as when I had last seen her, no older or thinner, the only difference being the worry in her eyes and on her mouth. Old instinct makes me want to go to her for comfort but then I see my father and I cease seeing her. He is lying with his eyes closed, covered up to his chin with a sheet. There is gray and white stubble on his sunken cheeks. The doctor says my father has pneumonia. He mentions a three-day high fever at which I put my hands in my pockets and push my nails into my palms.

Kawsar says quickly, "I only found out this morning."

The doctor goes on: prescription, medication, weakness, rest.

"When will he be discharged?" My voice shakes a little. It is from anger but the doctor assumes otherwise. He blinks, perhaps in an effort to look warmer.

"Tomorrow morning," he says.

After he leaves, Kawsar, my mother, and Meena look at me, almost fearfully, as if expecting a hearing for accountability led by me, the aggrieved.

"Three days?" I hiss at my mother. "You should have called me the moment he got sick. The very moment."

She shifts her jaw—a tiny movement—and her face hardens. Now she is the person I remember from when I was a child.

"I had no reason to call you. I have Kawsar. And you are here now because you were *called*, so what are you complaining about?" She says the word called in a mocking manner, almost spitting it out.

I jab a finger in the air toward her. "He is ill because of you."

"Go home, Baadal. You do not live here anymore. You are just a visitor."

Kawsar looks at the floor. "You're going to wake him up."

We have been speaking in low growls through gritted teeth and in whispers, but still my father stirs. We fall silent. I look around our little area, cast in greenish light. "I'm going to stay right here." I lower myself onto the floor, make a pillow of my arm, and close my eyes.

I wake up sometime in the night to see Meena and my mother in the corridor outside the ward, stretched out on chairs, head to head.

———

Meena is brisk and efficient when we are back. She takes down the sign she had quickly brought out and hung on the door when we were leaving for the hospital. It says, BEAUTY PARLOR CLOSED BECAUSE OF EMERGENCY IN HUSBAND'S FAMILY.

"When did you get this made?" I ask, falling onto the mattress.

"When I first opened the parlor. Naseema baji's son wrote it for me."

She dusts the chair, the table and the mirror. She dips a rag into a bowl of water and wipes her face clean. She gives me a glance then moves over to the stove. I sit up when she shakes my shoulder. "Drink the tea. It will freshen you. Then go to the restaurant."

It is hard for me to reestablish my old rules. I don't know if I believe in them anymore. What had they done for me? The money that I had carefully hidden in an inside pocket in my vest and brought to the hospital had not been enough. My mother had to make a phone call to her sister to arrange for the rest. And then there had been the question of who will stay with my father. He refused to go anywhere but back to his room. So it was arranged that Kawsar will sleep there on weeknights after his work, my mother will spend time with him during the day, and I will take my turn at the end of the week, the fewest hours of any of them.

I am extraneous. I am not needed.

But because having a place of my own and food on the table are habits that are necessary to maintain, and because I do not want Kawsar or Karim or Chacha Ameer or anyone else to buy my father's medication, I create new rules to strictly follow, to keep life stable once more. I don't fall asleep before saying a dua for the people I know in a particular order, first for my father, then my mother, then my two dead sisters, the older one first then the second one, Nabeela khaala, then Meena, Juman and Kawsar. Very soon I add Nabeela khaala's deceased husband and her living sons to this list. I collect every last crumb of food from my plate. I wipe the glass of the mirror from top to bottom before I look into it. When black spots appear on it, I rub hard at them but they don't go away. They make my jaw look diseased. I use the can of hairspray from Meena's parlor table but still they are there. I am nervous all day. Two days later the mirror is clear again. "What happened to the spots?" I ask. "This is a new one," Meena says, keeping her eyes on her needle.

Once, though, I make an error.

Jaafar offers me a new type of pill, a little cheaper than what I buy from him. "It melts all the body's aches away, makes it good as new," he says. I tell him no. He says, "Because you are my good, old friend, I will give this to you for free." So I take it. Sometime later, a song comes on the radio and Jaafar says, "Let me show you how to dance to this." I inch my way out from behind the reception desk and move my arms and torso the way my good friend does. When the song ends he stands under the yellow light, panting and shining. "This next one is even better," he says. And he is right.

It is after this that my father quickly becomes weaker. It takes longer and longer for him to get up from his bed. When I realize what I have caused, for a whole week I give my lunch to a child and go hungry myself as penance for that extra pill.

He begins to mention my mother every time I go to see him. He points out the clothes she has washed and mended for him. He moves a bare foot over the floor and tells me that she cleaned the room. He says, "Your mother does so much." He is easily irritated: the haleem I bring for him tastes bland; the colors in the TV are too bright. He does not want to me to go with him when he needs to use the bathroom. He wants me to stay in the room if he needs to sleep for a little while. Once, to lighten his mood, I ask him, "What will happen to you if I step outside?" And he points at the chair and says, "Just stay. Just stay." I do as he says, even after he says that my mother's care and devotion are incomparable and I am left to feel like a small, chastised child. I coax him into sitting outside; I make sure his feet are not covered by the blanket because he likes the feel of air on them; I watch the news with him, sometimes pretending to take a stance opposite his just to get him to sit up and loudly explain to me why I am wrong. I bring him a different saalan to try, tearing the naan into thin halves and breaking up those sections into small pieces. It becomes a habit for him to say, as I put on my shoes and pack up my clothes, "You should see your mother. I hope you are going to see your mother."

One of these times I do make a stop on the way to the bus, but it is to Darya Park. New benches and flowerbeds line the pathways from recent renovations. My father told me about some people who strongly objected to the practice of seclusion by the river and had driven through the Town, announcing through a loudspeaker that seeking atonement in the privacy of one's home was a far superior way of life. They walked into the park and gently but firmly told the people there to pack up and return to their homes. Almost in tandem with this, a cleanup crew from the City arrived and removed all traces of strings that had tied bedsheets to trunks, and collected any rosaries or booklets left behind. Still, sometimes a small group or two goes there, but they try to do it in secret.

At the park I see someone who looks like Juman but I am not sure. This man is lean in a strong way and has no hair on his head or face. Also, he is clean. He is sitting cross-legged, talking to a small group around him. Every few seconds they nod, gently and peacefully, like grasses in a soft breeze. I shift a little closer, hoping he will look up, but he doesn't. I think his voice is like Juman's. Without thinking, I pull out all of my money—a few currency notes and some coins—walk to him, and put them in his hand. I don't look into his face, and I don't stop to hear him speak.

℃Ↄ

My father dies a few weeks later. He passed away in his sleep, Kawsar says on the phone, and for a moment a calm washes over me. I say to my friend, in my false state of peace, "Well, that is one chapter closed for good." In the masjid in the Town I wash my father's body. Kawsar and my cousins help me. They lift his head and turn him on his side as I cover him with the shroud. Inside the hall of the masjid, there are a lot of rows of men praying for my father, and, afterward, there are a lot of carriers for his coffin. When we are back in the house that used to belong to both my mother and father, people come to me with wet eyes and say he was a good man, and I, dry-eyed, just nod. They trickle out slowly until there is more silence than talk. Asma and Meena collect dirty teacups and glasses and wash them in the kitchen. I have only spoken once to my mother since getting here. It was when, upon seeing me, she stumbled into my body and I held her, briefly. She now sits on the sofa, holding the hand of Juman's mother on one side and my aunt's on the other. A woman called Noor sits close to her feet. They are comforting my mother, and suddenly I feel distant and sickened. It is as if she never made my father want to leave, as if neither she nor I ever left, as if we should be allowed to grieve like regular people.

Karim finds me in a corner of the scrubby lawn, smoking a cigarette. It is many hours since the start of the day and his white shalwar qameez still looks clean, the sleeves rolled up to the middle of his forearms, a watch with a thick black strap and blue-gray dial full of tiny numbers and tinier letters wrapped around his wrist. Keeping his voice low, head bent toward me even though I am probably only an inch shorter than him, he tells me that he has paid off the grave-digger as well as given a little extra to the graveyard caretaker to make sure he keeps Uncle's grave neat. *So many mentions of the word grave,*

I think. I mumble my thanks and add that I will be sure to pay him back within a month, two at the most. But both of us know that the cost of burying my father was a staggering amount. Still, Karim nods as if he believes me.

"You should get back to work as soon as you can. It is the only thing that helps," he says.

I remember then that he too has a father who is now dead.

Later that afternoon, the whine of jet engines gradually fills the sky. We go up to the roof to see them. Five fighter planes fly over our heads, releasing blue, green, red, white, and pink smoke in the sky. In the morning, Juman comes by with breakfast and the newspaper. On an inside page is a small photograph of the planes. The caption says that the government surprised the Town with an airshow to display their support of us people on the far margins of the City, to show us we have not been forgotten.

∽

On Sundays there is quiet in the Colony, well past noon, but that is not what helps me sleep. I swallow one of the pills—the ones to guarantee rest as opposed to the ones that guarantee wakeful-ness—and I don't wake up until three, sometimes after that. It is spring now but I am almost always cold. I wear my sweater so often I have worn out the elbows. Meena doesn't ask to go anywhere, hardly ever. She understands, I think. So sometimes when she says to me let's watch this movie, or let's watch that program, I feel very bad and do not say no.

One afternoon, I open my eyes from my slumber on the sofa to a picture on the screen of a narrow street and a row of tired-looking homes. I recognize a building. My old school. And now there is the mural of Darya Park, the paint faded and flaking. For a moment

I feel just a little bit sad but I know it is just me being tired; I am glad when a woman with a microphone starts talking. "This once-thriving school now stands empty. The people wait for water, but the grounds have dried up and there has been no sign of rain for months now."

I become aware of Meena sitting by my feet, also watching. Her mouth is open, probably in surprise. I look at the TV again. Shops, a few wells. The camera moves across faces of people sitting on the side of a street or walking aimlessly, focuses on a small child wearing a long qameez with no shalwar, rolling a tire. And now there is the park, and the river. Only it really is a thin, gray-brown stream, with barely a current. Juman used to call it an intestine.

"That's my river," Meena points, wonderment in her voice.

On the browning, sparse grass near the water there are campers. The mic woman goes toward them and stops by an old woman. She says, "Drought must have been affecting your family for years, yet you have not moved away. How do you manage in the face of such adversity?" The old woman starts to explain about the cost of misdeeds and miracles. Other people begin to gather around them. They look derelict and lost. The interviewer nods a few times attentively then puts a hand on the old woman's hand and says, "Amma, my prayers are with you, and please keep me in yours." Then she delicately steps away from the crowd and speaks into the lens, "These people are a part of us. This land is part of our land. If you have gently used items of clothing to donate, please bring them to the address below." A list of names starts scrolling up as a flute plays a melancholy tune. When the last name disappears from the screen, Meena says, "I thought the river looked nice."

⁍

My father died without knowing how much I owed my mother's family. He would never know the debt his death put me in. My aunt would never question what she gave me as a loan, and maybe her sons would think the way she does, but I need to clear it up, to pay my debts. I find Karim at his house and hand him an envelope; there are only a few notes inside.

"I'll pay back a little every month."

He says, "Come on, you're like a brother."

"Well. I know that of course."

But I am not, of course.

ⁿ

I should be dreaming about my father. Instead, last night, I dreamed that my mother was looking for me, eyes and nostrils wide with determination, her straight eyelashes like sharp little sticks. We were in a city I did not recognize; yellow-brown buildings, donkey carts, minarets in the distance, a cloudless summer sky. In the dream, I always managed to stay around the corner, a few steps away from her, afraid but calm. I was a young man and she was an old mother. She was nimble in her anger and I was old with fear.

I have told Meena only one story from when I was very little. I don't remember what it was that I had done to make my mother extremely upset with me, but one of her arms was bleeding slightly. I remember her lifting me up in her arms, a move which surprised me. She told me we were going to play and right away I was warmed. We left the house and she walked until we had left our street and gone into another then another.

"Where are we going?" I asked her.

"I don't know."

"Are we getting ice cream?"

"No."

I don't think she walked a long distance. We reached a small seesaw, and I wriggled to get down. I remember there was nobody else there. My mother put me on one end of the seesaw and turned around and began to walk away.

"Push me," I called out to her.

She did not stop. I sat on the hard wooden seat for what felt like a long time, and eventually I tried puckering my mouth to see how sad I was, and I realized I could cry. I had not been doing it for long when I saw a man running up the street toward me. It was my father. He picked me up without a word and took me back home.

When I remember that evening, when I remember that once someone chose to save me, I feel, for a few moments, that my life and I can be mended, even though the memory of that man in the dark doesn't bring me remorse but only a recollection of the slippery-smoothness of a little foil wrapper of the candy that I pulled from his hand; the hiddenness of the moon; the warmth of the air. Even though I cannot find a way out of this cycle of keeping and owing.

☙

Meena and I are sitting under a tree in the park in the mausoleum grounds. There are gray clouds in the sky, and we are ready with our flimsy umbrellas in case it starts to rain. But for now, we are eating grapes and leaning against the hard trunk. Earlier, we walked barefoot on the cool white marble, shoes in our hands. We are here because Meena asked me several times lately if I was all right, if there was something wrong with the food, and if there was nothing wrong with the food then why did I forget I was eating it in the middle of our meals. So this morning I made sure I smiled and said to her, let's do something different this Sunday. And it has made me happy, I think. Meena is looking at me again, so I smile.

❦

I fall into a heavy sleep. I am with a young boy. We are standing next to the River, waiting for Juman. I can tell the boy wants to test the water with his foot. Juman says we can sit by the trees. He tells us the River has recently been fed because of a short rainfall. He had heard the water come down and he had made his way here in the soft black of the early morning and watched the River, lying twisted in its bed, its whole body a mouth, receiving. He had sat by its side and clapped and cheered. Then Juman opens a book and reads to me and the boy: rivers are born from snow and ice from mountains; rain makes rivers fatter; some rivers are thousands of centuries old. Juman's reading turns into a recitation. I realize it is a list of names of people who have died. At the sixth name he looks at me and says, This is the man with the hole in the head. My breath becomes constricted and my eyes struggle to open.

I wake up with the sound of my heart beating in my ear. Some kind of lit-up disc is sliding across the sky, the moon or the sun, I am unsure. I cannot afford to stay awake but my skin is sticking to the mattress and my head feels as though it has caught on fire. I turn to ask Meena to check if I am sick but she is asleep in a tight little ball, her back to me. I put my hand on my forehead but cannot tell if I have a fever. I reach for the little envelope of pills, the ones for sleeping. There are only ten left. Jafar got switched to the morning shift some time ago, the same time that I became careless about rationing the pills. I've had to go down from three pills to one and then half, scared of what will happen the day I have none in the envelope. I cannot remember going to bed or how many hours I have spent on it. I have only been able to sink into unconsciousness a few minutes at a time, interrupted by chaotic dreams about my father, Kawsar, Chacha Ameer, people I don't know. The worst are the ones about my mother. Now she is flying, now she is walking away from me. Now she is speaking urgently into my ear but I cannot understand her. I wake up angry, grinding my teeth.

I put on my shoes and go outside. There is early light in the sky, and that surprises me. I have missed the night shift. The main road is not quite full yet. I walk next to people moving their legs faster than I am. A billboard looms closer and closer. There is a woman on it wrapped completely in fabric, only her eyes looking out. I pass underneath her, stumbling over a brick in the path. The corrugated iron wall on my left ends and I pause there, looking down an avenue of trees and lampposts and parked cars.

At the other end is a tall building whose front is all glass. A guard stands at a pair of doors, holding a gun. They keep parting to let people in; a woman, then two men, then two women and a man. They look shiny, awake. Some of them are still getting out of their cars, their doors opening with rich little sounds. I become aware of the guard looking toward me at the same time that I feel my stomach contract in a spasm. Clutching it, I dart across the avenue entrance to the wall on the other side. I am almost doubled over, eyes watering. The wall ends and I step into the space behind it. Here the ground is covered with rubber tires and prickly shrubs and plastic bags. I lower my pants and crouch behind a bush, praying that nothing happens. And nothing does; I hold it all in. My insides untwist and I get up slowly.

In these moments it is as if I have crossed permanently to another side, firmly established what side of a particular wall I will always be forced to return to. I push through a crowd at a bus stop and walk underneath trees that are so old their wide trunks have become a muted, stately gray. I rub my eyes; they are itchy with tiredness and fumes. I nip the ends of my fingertips, a recent habit, but there isn't much feeling in them. I see with surprise that the sky has become lighter. I stand on the footpath, head spinning slightly. I am thirsty.

The air from a passing truck dries my sweat. I could step down onto the road in front of something like that. This is where drivers put on speed because they want to get through the signal before it turns red. It is a good place to be reckless and keep the blame away from anyone else, my mother, or Meena, or any cousin, or cousin's child, or old friend. I inch forward until half of my shoes are over the yellow-painted edge and wait for a truck to come up the road. Motorcycles, cars, little vans pass by me. Rickshaws and more motorcycles. I wait and breathe in the exhaust of everything and still no truck appears. Somewhere above me or behind me the sun comes up fully and the sky turns the palest blue in an instant. I become aware of the billboard with the picture of the woman in the fabric, her face now lit up with sunlight, gray-painted eyelids and brown eyes the only uncovered parts of her face. Had I passed this place before, or is this a different location? I am confused, trying to understand, looking into those irises.

The sudden, growing, deep bellow of a truck horn close by startles me, and I lose my balance. In that second my own and someone else's instincts try to jerk my body back, but I only have an intention not to die, and the stranger only has a weak grasp on the back of my shirt. For an instant, I am enveloped by sounds—the horn, the screams, the machinery of the truck—and then I see the house of my aunt, and the front door opening.

RAHEELA, 1998

THERE ARE THREE OF US IN THE HOUSE. Meena, Nabeela, and I. Four when Aleena comes to stay. She can spend as many days in this house as she likes, I don't mind. Nabeela says I will feel differently if Aleena ever stays more than three nights in a row, but I don't think so. She is clean, she does not talk much, and her name is like my little sister's. Besides, the longer Nabeela stays the more I want my friend around.

Nabeela says she is here because she is bored with the City, but I know the real reason; she thinks I have become incapable of taking care of myself ever since Masood died. The first time she stayed was after Baadal's father died. Then she had gone back to the City, to her home and her bed and her carpets and her fridge, and it is true, I had been angry that she left, but I got used to her absence soon enough. In fact, I was thankful for it. I did not even miss her when I tripped on a loose brick outside and fell on the ground and bruised my eye and chipped a tooth. For a second time, it was Aleena who found me and helped me up and tried to do useless things to bring down the swelling. In all of that, I might have thought about my sister maybe once, but no more.

She came back just a few days after my fall, before my eye healed. She brought suitcases and boxes and sat in the middle of the liv-

ing room and took out toothpaste tubes, toothbrushes, jars of talcum powder and night creams, and meters and meters of unstitched
shalwar qameez cloth, making little sounds and exclamations. From
another box, like a magician, she pulled out bedsheets, towels, and
a thin blanket. I felt embarrassed at my sister's complete lack of tact,
displaying her things in front of someone as poor as Juman's mother.
I said to Nabeela that I did not remember inviting her to move in.
She said she knew that, it wasn't as if she had received a card with her
name engraved upon it, now or for my second wedding. Then with
great calm and conviction she took her own suitcase into Baadal's
room and put away her things. On her way to the kitchen she saw
the beige sweater Masood liked and said, "You are not going to start
wearing that now, are you?"

"I am not crazy."

"You did want to bury him in it."

"It is still cold."

And then, when days and days passed and the sight of her clothes
hanging out to dry, mixed up with mine, became an ordinary sight,
I knew she was not going to leave. I got used to her bringing me tea
and I let her answer the door. The milkman, the vegetable seller, the
paper collector, I let her haggle with them all. I even let her deal with
the whole Meena situation, when she appeared on a very hot afternoon and burst into tears. I stood back and watched while Nabeela
led her in and sat her on the sofa. Juman's mother stood in a corner,
her big eyes darting from person to person.

I don't think it was unreasonable of me to be upset that Meena
had not brought Baadal with her, and I said as much to her. But
Nabeela jumped off her chair as if electrocuted and took me into the
kitchen and told me I must be nice to my son's wife, and she began
to cry as she spoke, which was also surprising and, if I am to be honest, a little irritating. I said that I was always nice to our visitors. To

prove it, I went right back to Meena and told her she could sleep in my room that night; I myself did not at all mind being in the living room on the floor. In fact, I found it very comfortable. Meena did not listen, but I was expecting that; she likes to do things her own way. She has been sleeping behind the sofa. Maybe she is waiting for Baadal to join her so that she can ask for the other room, the one he used to be in. In that case, Nabeela would have to shift in with me. A horrible thought.

Every now and then my sister says, "Let us have something nice to eat!" and tries to make sweet paratha like our mother used to once upon a time, but she is not very good at it. I ask her why she wastes good flour and she says I should be quiet and eat my food. She complains I am getting too thin and checks my plate after every meal. She also nags me about my hair and my clothes; it is endless. She spent six whole days trying to talk me into letting her and Meena shampoo and cut my hair. I finally gave in, mainly to shut her up. I stood very still in the bathroom as she rinsed my hair. Aleena was a few steps behind her, holding a towel.

"Those chemicals you just emptied onto my head cannot be good for me," I told my sister. "I always use soap. Nothing wrong with soap."

"This is better." Nabeela put the towel over my shoulders and spread my hair over it. "Now walk carefully. I don't need you slipping and breaking a bone."

"Look at all the water you wasted. You kept pouring and pouring, all because of that shampoo. Let go of my arm, I can walk."

She settled me onto a chair in the living room. There were pages from an old magazine spread on the floor by my feet. My sister, always present, muttered about coloring my gray hair while Meena combed it, very slowly, as if afraid to break it. She asked me to lower my head, speaking so quietly I could hardly hear her. I did as she said, looking down at photos of movie stars and singers. I had forbidden Meena from cutting off more than two inches; my hair should still come down to my waist, the way Baadal and his father were used to seeing.

Fingers replaced the grip of the comb, then scissor blades rasped through. Comb, fingers, blades. Meena moved to stand in front of me, now holding my head, now moving the comb down the left. She was breathing with her mouth open, like children do when working at something difficult. I searched my mind for a memory from childhood to match what was happening, sisters and friends taking care of each other, but there was nothing like that there. I did not know the woman near me. I had not liked looking at her. Once, a long time ago, I had not let her enter my house, and she and my son had had to go. Grief roared through my chest and my stomach like a bolt of lightning, and my head jerked away. Meena put her hands on it and stood for a moment, her scissors at rest, the two of us only breathing. The air in front of me became filled with the smell of soap from her shirt, and the heat from the lightning slowly left my body and my face.

When Meena was finished, Nabeela held up a small mirror and I turned my face from side to side. I liked my haircut. Aleena squatted down and carefully folded the hair-covered papers.

Nabeela gets irritated if I ask her to call Baadal more than three times in a day. "He doesn't have his own phone, Raheela," she says with a loud, gusty sigh. "But I haven't spoken to him for so long," I complain, and she reminds me that I have. She says, "You talked to him just a few days ago. Here, look, this looks like a nice program to watch."

———

My sister is full of busy movements, walking about with her feet in house slippers, her hands carrying or mending things, or on their way to. I cannot recall the exact day that she started bringing home the grocery, or took over the kitchen, or became in charge of the cleaning routine. In front of her I have to appear occupied; if she catches me doing nothing she shakes her head and says, "Staring at the wall again?" and hands me a qameez or a pillowcase with holes and tells me they need mending. I think she rips them up herself. I cannot tell her that it isn't the wall I am looking at. I am looking at Baadal.

Every week she tries to make me go with her to visit people. It seems that someone is always coming back to the Town, or leaving it, or dying in it, or being born in it, or getting married in it. She has learned to leave me alone when I start humming loudly, because she knows that if she goes on I would go into my room and lock the door. At these times Meena disappears into the lawn, but Aleena stays, silent and placid. Sometimes, to spite my sister, I say, "I am only going because *she* would like me to go," pointing in Aleena's direction. Then, because I have given in already, I let my sister lay out my clothes for me, even the undergarments.

Sometimes, when my sister is not chattering near me and I am able to be alone, I like to pick out an image in my mind from when it was me, Baadal, and Masood—his father, my husband—and I rearrange a part of it. I picture my son on a day when he was very young. I am cutting his hair and he is sitting in a chair. I imagine he is not making whimpering sounds like a frightened puppy, and that I do not pinch his face in my hands and tell him to be quiet. And then when he tries to wrest the scissors from my hand and the sharp points puncture the skin on my arm and he runs away, I imagine that I do not roar and run after him with those scissors, the points of the blade in the direction of his back, or his open screaming mouth when he turns his head to see how far I am. And when I manage to grab him and he kicks and screams, I tell him I am going to take him outside to play. I carry him to a seesaw, and here I change the pictures again: I seat him on the wooden square at one end, put my hands over his thin, dry, small ones, and push down slowly.

I don't go farther back than this in my mind; beyond that boundary of time there is a very large, blurred jungle with a sister and a brother in it.

Yesterday Nabeela said an old husband and wife had opened up their house again.

"They are done with the City," she said, taking out bananas and apples from a bag. I had never bought bananas and apples. "But their daughter will stay. Her name is Aab. She runs a school there, they told me."

I picked up a plastic bottle filled with a thick reddish substance.

"That is ketchup," Nabeela said. "Very tasty."

I remembered it then, the sharp taste of it, a potato chip dipped and fed to me by a boy years and years ago. "I know what it is," I snapped.

"Anyway, I told them you and I will visit tomorrow morning." She paused in her task and looked at me. She expected an argument from her irritable, ignorant sister, but from the corner of my eye I saw Baadal slip into the room in his starched school shirt and navy-blue pants pressed so well the crease down each leg was like a knife edge. His hair was parted so neatly it was as if he had done it with a ruler. I sat a little straighter, chose the most sensible fruit I could think of, and said to my sister, "Yes, let's take some bananas to them. I have been wondering about those people."

———

I am on my chair in the lawn, not wanting to be disturbed for a long time; a whole day at least, two if I am lucky, the way I used to be able to before my sister moved in, but I hear her footsteps behind me and the sound of a chair being dragged. She sits down with a sigh.

"They found a body in the river."

I do not look up from the cushion cover I am sewing for Aleena. I hope she comes by; I have not seen her these last few days. Maybe if I keep my eyes on my work and do not answer, Nabeela will go away. But she goes on talking.

"It is an old woman. They think she had been there three days at least. Face and arms and all parts bloated and unnatural. Her poor son had to identify her. Aleena was there as well; she ran to the river when the news got out about a body. She was scared it would be her son."

Nabeela's voice is sad, like autumn smokiness. I hum a song I once heard on TV.

"I heard she fainted with relief when she saw it was someone else."

When she gets up and finally does go away, I find myself unable to care about the cushion.

A few nights ago I saw Masood in a dream. He told me there is water in the earth over which our house stands.

"Beneath the foundation?" I asked him.

"Underneath the lawn," he said.

I have kept this piece of news to myself. If I tell it to Nabeela she will say I am just feeling sad about everyone's deaths, and make me a cup of tea. I return to the well. I dig all night until my arms feel stiff as the wooden handle.

It is unfortunate that Nabeela finds me asleep outdoors before Aleena does. It is from her shouting that I wake up. Even when we are inside and I am sitting up in a chair and she is walking over with tea and bread, her voice remains high and quivering. "I saw you lying on the ground—what were you doing there? Have you completely lost your mind? You have soil in your hair." She wipes dirt from my hair, my face. She shakes her head. "It will take all morning to untangle these knots. And what if you had fallen into that hole in the ground? I don't know, I don't know anything about your life. If you pass out like that again I'll have to take you to a doctor."

I exchange a look with Aleena. She does not mention that this is not the first time I have fallen asleep or fainted in the little dirt lawn.

I am made to rest all day, and I have a short visit from my mother and my son. I wake up with my heart beating too fast. I run to the phone and dial the number I taped on the wall with my son's number on it. His landlord's child says hello. I ask for Baadal, and wait, rocking on my heels. It is the child's mother's voice I hear on the phone. He isn't here, she says patiently, Baadal is gone. She sounds tired so I put down the receiver. An hour later my hunger to try him returns. This time the woman answers first. Behind her, a movie or a drama plays loudly.

"It is you again," she says loudly, her voice croaking. "Amma, it is ten in the night. Do your tasbeeh, say a dua for your son, pray he gets to go to Jannat and you meet him there."

"It is urgent, it won't take more than a minute."

"Urgent, urgent, always it is urgent. It is too late now, call in the morning."

"And what if I am sick? What if I am dying?" I am angry and paralyzed with my inability to reach my son.

"You sound perfectly healthy to me, Amma." With a loud click the receiver is put down.

Unhappily, I go back to my room.

The next night I try the main door but Nabeela has locked it. I cannot find the key anywhere. I kneel by her sleeping form and speak into her ear. "I want to go out."

Her eyes fly open as she gasps. Then she sees it is me. "It is dark. You will fall and break your neck."

So from then on I stop eating and drinking. There is no point when I cannot go to the well to see my mother, or my husband, or any other surprise visitor, and cannot speak when I like on the phone. I only eat a little bit when hunger becomes too hot in my stomach, and only when Aleena sits with me. Both she and I can wait and wait before that stage arrives, and Meena never eats more than strictly necessary, and Nabeela becomes very upset.

One day I find myself being woken up in the bathroom. Over my face is Nabeela's round one and Aleena's pinched one. In the living room stands a man I don't recognize. He was brought in off the street to break open the door, Meena explains quickly. Nabeela does not speak her usual volumes of words the rest of that day. It is peaceful like that, and I tell her so. But it is also strange, like the sudden quiet after the TV has been turned off.

At the end of that week, Baadal comes to the house. I let Meena sit next to me while I tell my son about the people I see down the well through the grating sometimes—my father, my sister, that boy called Juman. "They are not always there. And I have yet to see my brother." I turn to Nabeela. "You will have to vacate Baadal's room now. You can sleep in my room, I suppose. Don't worry, nobody dead will visit you there—you're not nearly interesting enough." I tell Baadal, "If you want you can see your friend, Juman. He's healthier, thank God, he used to be such a stick. Got all his teeth back too." I pause to drink soup from a spoon someone holds to my lips.

ACKNOWLEDGMENTS

For ALL THE PEOPLE involved in the making of this book: thank you.

14 Day

- - NOV 2023

CL